RHYMING RINGS

Also by David Gemmell:

RHYMING RINGS

DAVID GEMMELL

This edition first published in Great Britain in 2017
by Gollancz

First published in Great Britain in 2017
by Gollancz
an imprint of the Orion Publishing Group Ltd
Carmelite House, 50 Victoria Embankment
London EC4Y 0DZ

An Hachette UK Company

1 3 5 7 9 10 8 6 4 2

A CIP catalogue record for this book
is available from the British Library.

ISBN 978 1 473 21994 6

Typeset by Deltatype Ltd, Birkenhead, Merseyside

Printed in Great Britain by CPI Group (UK) Ltd,
Croydon, CR0 4YY

www.orionbooks.co.uk
www.gollancz.co.uk

INTRODUCTION

I can't help wondering how things would have gone if David Gemmell had taken this path. After all, Michael Connelly was a reporter in LA before he turned to crime fiction. This reminds me strongly of Connelly's books, or perhaps an early Lee Child. The style is so stripped down, it's almost a Dick Francis or a Raymond Chandler – but it has some of the elements that came to be Gemmell's hallmarks – deft strokes of character, the insecurity of youth, the ageing warrior, forgiving women, the clear-eyed comprehension of evil. He wrote women with warmth and understanding and love – but he wrote men as well as anyone you'll ever read.

The book ahead is set in the eighties and the way the characters talk and act reflect that decade. In *The Merchant of Venice*, Shylock is treated cruelly, and yet Shakespeare made his audience feel pity – so that in the final reckoning, they knew to stand on his side. Gemmell does the same thing here. The reader knows from the start that Mr Sutcliffe is a good man and strong. There always was a sort of decency in Gemmell's books, an understanding of failure and weakness – and how that differs from true cruelty. There are horrific crimes here, but he does not revel in them. Nor does he pass over them. His is a light touch.

Over the centuries, a number of authors from Cicero to

Luther, to Benjamin Franklin and Mark Twain, are credited with one line – that they were sorry for the length of a piece, but lacked the time or skill to make it shorter. It rings true. It is no easy thing to write as clearly and concisely as Gemmell could, believe me. His is the style of a man who wants to communicate, rather than impress. This is unornamented, clear, forceful writing. George Orwell would have loved his books, I think.

It is the difference between a storyteller and a Booker prize winner. Now there's nothing wrong with Booker prize novels – we all have wobbling tables, or draughts coming in under the door. Yet humanity needs stories and Gemmell could tell them. He is the enigmatic figure in the big coat who comes to the fire and weaves tales – and is gone in the morning.

The thing about those tales is that they can entertain or frighten, but all the time, at the heart of them, there is a set of values. The best tales make us gasp or laugh, but we also come away with a better idea of courage, or self-sacrifice, or ambition, or even evil. Such things need to be described sometimes, for good and bad, for us all to know what they look like.

I'm not at all surprised Gemmell was drawn to write about crime. Crime fiction is always about good and evil – and no matter how it seeks to shock or disturb the reader, we know Sherlock or Poirot, Bosch or Miss Marple or perhaps Jack Reacher will defeat that evil in the end. Probably. These days, not always. We like to frighten ourselves as well.

It is hard to read an ending, though I actually read this one at two in the morning. I can wonder what great crime series would have come from David Gemmell if he hadn't been drawn another way. Yet we would have lost Waylander and John Shannow, Gian Avur and Culain, Parmenion and Druss. I introduced my son to those last year – and he loved them, of course.

So read this as a straight crime novel – and it will sweep you up into the storm. Or read it in the words of Tennyson, for 'the sound of a voice that is still'. Either way, it has been a privilege.

Conn Iggulden

The driver was whistling as the car turned into Carlisle Road, and he saw the moon's twin shining on a large puddle ahead. He sent the nearside wheel slicing through the water, slashing spray into the trees beside the road. The man chuckled, feeling like a little boy again, riding his bike down the long hill to the pretend lake that gathered there after the rain. Just as he reached it he would lift his legs to the handlebars and watch as the water rose on either side of him like two triumphal arches.

As he swung the steering wheel to glide the saloon car into Controse Avenue, a shadow moved in front of him. He hit the brake and spun the car just as the child's bicycle scraped the front wing. As soon as the car screeched to a halt, the driver scrambled out. The boy had fallen into the gutter and was picking himself up, his eyes large and frightened. The driver ran to him.

The boy looked at the man – who was tall, his hair close-cropped and neat – and searched his eyes for signs of anger. There were none. The man sighed in relief as he saw the boy was unhurt.

'You all right, son?'

'Yeah.'

'You shouldn't be out this late. And you ought to have lights on that bike.'

'It's a BMX. They don't have lights.'

'Well, be careful. You nearly died just then.'

'I will. Sorry.'

He ruffled the boy's hair. 'The man who never made a mistake never made anything. But learn from it.' He grinned at the boy, who mounted the BMX and set off at speed. The man shook his head and continued the drive home.

Once there, he made a telephone call, ate a meal of cheese on toast, showered and settled down to watch a movie on video. It was an old favourite, but he never tired of it: *On Golden Pond* with Katharine Hepburn and Henry Fonda. This time he shed no tears.

He switched off the TV and thought of the boy, and how close he'd come to killing him. He shivered. His own bike hadn't been a BMX – they didn't have those fifteen years ago. His had been a Raleigh tourer. Secondhand but beautifully maintained. Dad had fixed it up a treat. He was good with his hands, loved to repair things. But some things couldn't be repaired. Especially when no one knew they were broken.

'Don't think about it,' he told himself. He walked to the cocktail cabinet and poured himself a gin.

At midnight, he showered and changed into a dark sweater, combat trousers and trainers. He took what looked like a black woollen hat from a desk drawer and walked outside to the garage. Lifting the up-and-over door, he climbed into the blue Sierra and switched on the ignition. He didn't like the car much. It was too heavy. 'You've been spoiled,' he said, thinking of his own vehicle's power steering. He wrenched the wheel and manoeuvred the Sierra out onto the drive, then returned to lock the garage.

It was a beautiful night. He drove across town until he reached the road parallel to his destination. He cut the engine, allowing the car to coast to a parking space near the corner. Scanning the nearby buildings, he saw no lights at the windows. He exited the car, keeping to the shadows until he reached the house. It, too, was dark.

From a leather pouch on his belt, he took a six-inch needle, which he rammed into a large cork. He placed it on the wall of the front garden then lifted his hands to his woollen hat and tugged. The hat stretched down into a balaclava mask, leaving only his eyes showing. Across the brow was a single word, neatly embroidered in white.

DEATH.

2

There is one word guaranteed to make any journalist reach for the wooden cross or the clove of garlic. It is rarely spoken in any newspaper office, as if it carries some mystical power and will cling to the walls like dry rot.

Ordinary.

The history of modern journalism has been a crusade to wipe the word from reality. A woman who raises her children well, despite the harshness of a life of poverty, becomes a 'supermum'. The pensioner who tackles the post-office robber is a 'have-a-go-hero'.

In the world of headlines, all of life's potent dramas are played out by special, and interesting, people.

That's the problem when writing about Ethel. How to convey, despite her powers, the very ordinariness that made her talents so unique. When I first met her, she was well into her sixties, with a face beautifully suited to her age, as if all her life she had waited for this moment to shine. There was no way Ethel could ever have been young. It just wouldn't have suited her.

Her home reflected her life: neat, tidy and peopled with tiny glass birds and animals, beautifully sculpted peacocks and glittering carriages drawn by impossibly skeletal horses. There was also the usual, mawkish, print of the crying child with the single tear drop on its well-scrubbed rosy face. You knew, without asking, that Ethel had no children.

But she had an enormous family. Not one regular resident of *Coronation Street, Crossroads* or *Eastenders* was not known intimately by Ethel. The Colbys, the Ewings, the Carringtons – all brought their troubles and woes into her dainty living room.

Do I sound as if I disliked her at first? Perhaps I did. Her ordinariness offended me, as if it had been created for that purpose. But I was different then. I knew so much more. I was gifted with an unreal understanding of all life's mysteries. I was the new generation, the one that would sweep away the stupidities of the past. There had been nothing like me in the history of the planet. I was the future.

I was also the star reporter on a weekly paper. No, let me rephrase that: I saw myself as the star reporter. The others lacked talent and inspiration. Of course they worked hard, but what did that mean? And they cared, about the town and the paper, but I had no use for that. I only cared about the most important being in the known universe. Me. The career of Jeremy Miller was off and rolling.

Which probably explains why, when the murders began that spring, it was Phil Deedes and Sue Cater who covered the stories, while the paper's 'star' reporter was sent to the Women's Institute meeting at Calver Hall to record for posterity who baked the cakes and who was thanked for the floral display.

That's where I first saw Ethel. The speaker, according to the neatly typed programme, was supposed to be Miss June Southfield, with a riveting talk and slide show on Ancient Rome. But she'd been struck down with flu, and instead we were to be treated to 'another hour with the always popular Ethel Hurst'.

People began digging into handbags and producing pens, lighters, compacts, medallions, earrings, brooches, whatever they had with them. I thought for a moment I was witnessing a bizarre, off-the-cuff bring-and-buy sale. Ethel's helpers moved around the audience collecting articles. A powerfully built lady with legs like tree trunks halted in front of me.

'Do you have an item, Mr Miller?'

'For what?'

'It will be returned,' she said, flashing her dentures. I reached into my pocket and came up with an old Zippo lighter my grandmother had kept since the war.

Ethel stood silently by the table at the front of the hall, waiting as the articles were placed on it in a neat line. She rubbed her hands together as if they were cold, then lifted a golden brooch. She closed her eyes.

'Ah,' she said, her voice deeper than I'd expected. 'Italy ... Venice, in fact. A lovely city. There is a dark-haired man, tall, very handsome, sitting at a round table. He's smiling. The sun is shining quite brilliantly as he reaches out his hand to the young lady beside him and gives her the brooch. It is a gift of love.' She opened her eyes. 'And it was given to you, Mrs Waters.'

The audience swung to stare at a large woman with blue-rinsed hair. She was nodding vigorously, and a tear could be seen on her cheek.

The star reporter felt a warm, comfortable feeling seep through him. Here was something better than gold. Here was a feature article. Perhaps even – praise be to the gods of journalism – a centre-page feature article.

I waited without patience for the elderly woman to reach the Zippo. At last, she lifted it. She put it down at once.

'A wartime find,' she said. 'Not a gift at all.' Then she moved on to a set of earrings. I was disappointed, wondering if she was merely a clever trickster after all. It wasn't difficult to see that the lighter was old.

At the end of the evening, after the obligatory – yet warm – applause, I made my way to the table and recovered my lighter. Ethel detached herself from a small group of women and approached me. Average height, slightly overweight and a little round-shouldered, she wore a dress of blue under a pink cardigan. Her hair was almost completely silver except at the temples, which still showed a mousy brunette.

'I'm sorry I could say so little about your lighter, young man. But you see, there was blood on it, and this isn't the sort of gathering where one should expound on violence.'

'Violence?'

'Three men owned it during the war. All died. The last married your grandmother. It was among the items sent to her.'

'I'm afraid you're wrong, Miss Hurst. My grandmother married an English seaman in 1944 or thereabouts. He only died last year.'

'Well, I have been wrong before,' she said. 'Excuse me.'

Tucking my notebook into my jacket pocket, I left the hall. Maybe not a centre-page article, then, but a small feature was still a possibility.

The pool car was a blue Fiesta with a sharp clutch. I could still smell Sue Cater's powerful perfume clinging to the upholstery. I lit a cigarette, vainly hoping the acrid smoke would push her presence from my mind. I knew I was charming, handsome, witty and an ideal lover. So why did Sue make me feel young, flash, clumsy and – worst of all – stupid?

I guess I knew the answer, but even 'star' reporters could be allowed a little self-delusion.

The following morning, I took my WI report to our news editor, Don Bateman. I didn't like him. The man wasn't even a has-been. He was a never-was.

'What do you think?'

'Not bad. Cut down the psychic element. Leaves you some interest for a feature. John could use a nice colour piece for page eight. Have a word with him about length. What time you seeing her?'

'I haven't made an appointment.'

'Might be a good idea. Where does she live?'

'I'm checking that now.'

'I thought you saw her last night.'

'She slipped away before I had a chance to talk to her.'

'Yeah,' said Bateman. 'That's the problem with pensioners – they move like greased lightning.' He shook his head.

'I'll find her.'

'Yeah. You're also down for Environment Committee tonight. Get in touch with Samuels at the Jam Factory. See what they've done about the smell.'

'We carried that story last week.'

'No? Really? Must have slipped my mind, superstar. You don't think the readers might be the teensiest bit interested to know whether any progress has been made? You don't think the matter might be raised tonight at the Environment Committee?'

That's the way he was. All the good humour of a burning hospital.

I left him then, to track down Ethel.

3

Now, for those of you who know nothing of West London, let me explain. It used to be a fine place to live. Then the Nazis dropped a few hundred thousand bombs on it. This caused some damage. After the war several hundred Nazi infiltrators took further revenge by burrowing their way into council offices and introducing vertical housing, dual carriageways and office blocks. Other sympathisers went into property speculation and forty years after the war Hitler had the last laugh. What emerged over those decades was enough sprawling, soulless, slate-grey concrete to engulf all community spirit. In its absence came the muggers and the criminals and all the vile dregs of a decomposing society.

True? Not exactly, but too close to the truth for any real comfort. Where once communities had existed in tight-packed terraces and all front doors were open, now every night was punctuated by the sound of the bolt slipping home, the lock turning, the chain rattling.

Some areas are better than others. Ethel Hurst did not live in one of them. I found her house next to a derelict factory in the shadow of a rusting iron bridge. Across the road was a grocer's store. I knew it was run by Asians because the windows were smashed despite the iron grille, and also because it was still open when I parked the Fiesta. It was not an area in which I would have left a car of my own.

Her house was of the terraced variety so popular now

with chartered accountants and record producers and described as 'charming' by estate agents who speak a different language from the rest of humanity. I locked the car and opened the green gate. There was a tiny front garden no more than six feet square which boasted quite the most beautiful roses. Not being a gardener, I couldn't name them then, but later I learned they were Peace – a subtle yellow with pink edging; Piccadilly – red and yellow; and Wendy Cussons – a glorious pinky-red with a perfume that, said Ethel, proved the existence of God.

Ethel opened the door and ushered me into a hallway so tiny even an estate agent would think twice before calling it 'charming'. Of all things, Ethel was wearing jeans and a chunky sweater.

'I must apologise for my appearance, Mr Miller, but these days I do try to dress for comfort when I'm home. Do sit down. Smoke if you wish.'

I eased myself back into a white vinyl armchair and she placed a 'charming' ashtray beside me on which there was room for the ash of a very short cigarette. I decided not to smoke. I pulled my notebook from my pocket, knocking the ashtray to the floor in the process. Ethel perched herself on the edge of the seat opposite.

'Your talent—' I said.

'A cup of tea,' she announced, rising and moving out of the room, returning seconds later with a tray laden with a silver teapot and two cups and saucers. She must have had them ready.

'Milk?'

'Yes, please, and two sugars. Your talent—'

'I'm sorry – I've forgotten the sugar.' She bustled out again.

In her absence, I caught my first glimpse of the grotesque

painting of the child with the tear in its eye. I remember sighing deeply as I stood and removed my coat. On the mantel shelf, above the coal fire, I noticed a photograph in a silver frame.

It showed a small man with a friendly face. He was dressed in a coat that had recently come back into fashion, and I guessed the picture was around thirty years old.

'My husband, Freddie,' said Ethel, returning with a jug of milk. 'Nice man. Everyone called him Feathers.'

'Why?'

'He bred whippets.'

'Your talent,' I began for the third time. 'How did you come by it?'

'I have always had it. Even as a child, though it is much stronger now than it was. Mr Sutcliffe says it is an earth magic. I rather like that. It is less ... sinister than some of the alternatives.'

'And you can tell where any object comes from?'

'No, of course not. Is the tea all right?'

'Very nice.'

'It's Earl Grey mixed with good old-fashioned English breakfast tea. I find it so refreshing.'

'What's the most exciting example you have of your ... talent?'

'Exciting? I don't think it has ever been exciting. What is this for, Mr Miller?'

'It's for a feature – an article for the local paper.'

'Oh, I don't want any articles. No, no! I thought you'd come to see me about your grandmother. Nice woman.'

'You know her?'

'Only through the lighter. She really should have told your grandfather about her first marriage, but things were different then, weren't they? Oh, I don't suppose you'd remember. But men were so rigid in their thinking.'

'I'm sorry, Mrs Hurst, but I don't know what you're talking about.'

'Go and see her. Ask her about Eddie. I am sure she'd love to talk about him.'

'But my article—'

'I remember when newspapers were nice things. When they told you all the good news and made you feel part of a community. Now it's all Aids and sex and crime. It's so unsettling. Like that poor woman who was murdered recently … Sinclair? It really is all too sad. I'm sure I would not like a story about me to be surrounded by such unpleasantness.'

'You won't be surrounded by it,' I said, wondering what on earth I was talking about. 'You'll be on page eight. That's a feature page. You'll have it to yourself.'

'I'm sure there are other interesting people to write about. Now put away your notebook and enjoy your tea.' The doorbell rang. Ethel rose.

'That will be Mr Sutcliffe,' she said. 'He's coming round to put up some shelves in the bedroom, for all my books. Such a sweet man.'

I drained the tea and stood, turning towards the door. Suddenly, an enormous shape loomed. Standing in the doorway was a giant with shoulders that touched the door frame on both sides. I looked up into dark eyes set into a jet-black complexion.

The giant stepped into the room. I hastily made way for him, sensing he would have walked through me if I didn't. As he passed me, I felt a shiver of fear that I couldn't explain. Ethel appeared behind him.

'Mr Miller, this is my neighbour, Mr Sutcliffe.'

'Pleased to meet you,' I said, not entirely truthfully. His lips twitched above his black and grey beard. I took it to be a friendly gesture. 'I must be going,' I said. 'Thank you, Mrs Hurst, for seeing me.'

'Not at all. But you be sure to speak to your grandmother.'

'I will. Goodbye, then. Goodbye, Mr Sutcliffe.' The giant's head gave an almost imperceptible nod.

I dreaded telling Don Bateman I'd lost the story, but at least with the Sinclair murder he would have other, more important matters on his mind.

4

I drove home through South Acton and turned into Avenue Road. Yet again, a lorry had parked in my space and I left the car some two hundred yards from my flat.

My landlady Mrs Simcox was still awake and, though I entered the building as silently as I could, she stepped into the hall and greeted me. An elderly woman and a drunk, she was always friendly, but somehow the sight of her unsettled me – this slender, bird-boned woman with dyed-black hair, white at the roots, clutching a tumbler of sherry. It wasn't the drink that bothered me, although she had an alarming habit of turning the gas on and forgetting to light the burner. It was her eyes: large, sad eyes, made all the more sorrowful by her perpetual smile.

'Hello, dear, been working late?'

'Yes, Mrs Simcox. How are you?'

'Never pays to grumble, dear. Would you like a cup of tea?'

'No thanks. I have to feed the cats, and then I'm going out again.'

'Another time, then,' she said, accepting defeat with the same smile and the same sorrowful look.

As I walked slowly up to my flat on the second floor, I promised myself, as I always did, that next time I would sit down and have a cup of tea with Mrs Simcox. I knew she was lonely, but I couldn't bear to share her burdens.

My cats began wailing the moment I walked in. I don't like cats. I never have. But they were dumped in the back garden in a sack. Three kittens left in a dustbin. Somehow, in a world plagued by starvation and war, it felt ridiculous to be as outraged as I was when I discovered them. After all, what difference did it make that three small animals had been sentenced to death so casually? I still can't answer the question. I remember dropping a black plastic bag into the bin and then seeing movement. I thought it was rats at first and my blood froze. I couldn't do anything. I wanted to lift out the canvas bag but fear stopped me. Then I heard the pitiful mewing and rushed off to fetch Mrs Simcox. She rescued them.

I kept them.

There were two black and white kittens, both female, and a white tom. I bought a large litter box and several tins of cat food, convincing myself I would find homes for them. But, as animals do, they forced their way into my affections and now I was stuck with them. I was determined not to name them. I had always felt uncomfortable when faced with pets with idiot names like Dopsy or Suki-tops. It sounded so ridiculous. I remember my father having to walk out into the backyard at night calling, 'Snowdrop, here Snowy, good girl!' Equally ludicrous were macho names like Fang and Bronco – my next-door-neighbours' Dobermans.

No, my cats would be nameless.

That decision lasted less than a fortnight. The first to earn his spurs, so to speak, was Rascal, the white tom, whose method of greeting me was to run at speed up my trouser leg and hang, wailing, from my jacket. As he grew larger and heavier, he did not wail alone. A rascal he was, and Rascal he became.

The second and third names were decided within another

two days. The smallest of the trio, black with a white face and blue eyes, was terrified of every sound. Turn on the television and she would rush to the bed and burrow under the duvet. She became Chicken, and I must admit to a greater fondness for her than the others. From the safety of my lap she would hiss and spit at the others, pretending great courage. But alone? Straight back under the duvet.

The last was Piddler, and she needs no explanation.

This was my family, sharing with me a three-room flat overlooking South Acton. The view was uninspiring. To the south, I could see the towering blocks of the nearest estate, dominating the skyline with their ugliness. Only at night did they achieve beauty, sometimes seeming to be vertical ships ablaze with deck lights, steaming out on a voyage to the stars. The front windows looked out on Avenue Road and down towards the town centre.

The flat itself boasted a large kitchen-breakfast room, a lounge and a tiny bedroom, curtained off from the lounge. I had a double bed then, which was gloriously wishful thinking. Under the bed were two cardboard boxes. One contained my collection of Spiderman comics; the other was a box of toy soldiers of the American Civil War. At the age of twenty-four, I still lined the soldiers up in rows and played at battles like Bull Run or Shiloh. My heroes were the Confederates. Not, I hasten to add, because I liked the idea of slavery. No, I just have a soft spot for losers.

It wasn't a bad flat. I guess I was happy there. I know the cats were.

Anyway, I fed them, cleared out the litter tray and changed into jeans and sweatshirt. Our editor was a nice, inoffensive guy, but he wouldn't allow jeans during office hours.

I wandered to the oval mirror above the blocked-up fire-place and checked out the face. I thought it looked pretty good, but the eyes in the mirror were mocking. Meeting that cynical gaze, I could understand why people didn't like me. I took my rechargeable razor and ran it over the faint stubble then splashed some Chanel cologne onto my cheeks. I didn't like the smell, but a barmaid told me one time that her boyfriend wore it and she thought it was a great turn-on. So far it hadn't worked for me.

Still, my mother liked it. And my Aunt Edna said it was sweet.

'Very nice, dear,' Aunt Edna said when I started using it. 'You won't stay lonely wearing that!'

'I'm not lonely,' I snapped. 'Who said I was lonely?'

'Just a slip of the tongue, dear.'

That was the trouble with living at home – everybody knew your secrets. That was why I got the flat. Now, after four months, I was still lonely, and sometimes I even missed Aunt Edna's spinsterish probings into my private life.

Silently, I descended the stairs.

'Have a nice time, Jeremy,' said Mrs Simcox, stepping into the hallway.

'You, too.'

'I always have a nice time.'

I didn't look at her eyes, just smiled and walked out to the Fiesta. With any luck, Sue Cater would be at the Six Bells, and it wouldn't do any harm to find out how the murder story was progressing.

I parked outside the pub and switched off the ignition. I glanced up. Those mocking eyes stared back at me from the rear-view mirror.

The pub was crowded, the noise unpleasant. A tinny cover version of an old Boy George single was competing with the electronic blipping of a fruit machine, the clinking of glasses and the patter of a dozen conversations. I thrust my body into the chaos and pushed towards the back of the lounge where Sue Cater was sitting with Phil Deedes and Don Bateman at a corner table. She looked up as I approached and gave me the merest glimpse of a smile. It was not welcoming. The other two acknowledged me and returned to their conversation. I pulled up a chair regardless. Bateman frowned and for a few seconds there was an uncomfortable hiatus – you couldn't call it a silence in those surroundings. Eventually, Bateman realised I was staying. He took a deep breath and switched his gaze to Sue.

'Do they have any theories as to why the stitching?'

'Nothing, Don. It's obviously a nutter.'

'What about witnesses?'

'Zero so far. He must have climbed in through the second-floor window at around two a.m. No one saw or heard anything.'

'Have you tracked down the ex-husband?'

'Yes. The police questioned him for over two hours. He won't talk to us.'

'What about friends?' asked Bateman, swinging to Deedes.

'Still working on it, Don. She's a local girl, Faraday School before it was turned into the King Fahad Academy. I'm checking her background. I've an interview tomorrow with her old English teacher – he's retired now, lives in Ealing.'

'Okay, we'll pick up the threads tomorrow. But I want some angles the nationals won't have, so no lineage sales. We write this ourselves.' He turned to me. 'You see the old lady who does tricks?'

'Yes. She wants time to think about it. What was that you said about stitching?'

Sue Cater stood and moved past me to the bar. Bateman glanced around the crowded lounge and lowered his voice. 'The killer stitched the victim's genitals together. He killed her with a spike in the back of the head, had sex with the corpse and then stitched her closed. Nice, eh?'

'Takes all sorts, I suppose,' I said, trying to be cool despite the shock to my system. Bateman swore. Deedes turned away.

Congratulations, Jeremy, I told myself. *Score one more point for stupidity.* Sue had returned with a vodka and tonic for herself and a lager for Bateman. Deedes was still nursing a half-pint of orange squash. I could feel the hot flush of anger on my face.

'I'll get my own,' I said.

'Why don't you do that?' she said. 'And find somewhere else to drink it.'

If I'd left then I would have earned some credit, for Bateman at least looked embarrassed. But I didn't. I calmly reached across the table, lifted Deedes's orange squash and splashed the remains into her face. Then I left.

I'd like to say that I felt better for allowing my anger to wash over me, but I didn't. I was hurt. Strange little word, isn't it? It never seems to convey, of itself, the searing, savage devastation that accompanies inner pain. I saw a man once, standing outside a house, thrashing a bouquet of roses against a wall. Red petals hung in the air alongside him, and he was crying and screaming. Inner pain changes the perspective. Ten minutes before that, those flowers had been beautiful to him. Now they were objects he needed to destroy.

I thought of him as I stood outside that pub, feeling the bitterness ripping at my insides. I knew what would follow. Self-loathing. The incident wasn't isolated. Flash, un-pleasant Jeremy Miller had gatecrashed a private meeting and made a suitably tasteless remark.

I walked to the car. Something moved behind me and I

swung around just in time to take Deedes's fist against my ear. I stumbled but didn't fall. Deedes was not a large man and he was dancing in front of me, fists raised, ready for combat. He reminded me of the monkeys in the old movies that held out cups as the organ grinder turned the handle.

'Come on then, you bastard!' he said.

I ignored him and unlocked the car door.

'You gutless chicken shit!' he yelled. Sue Cater was standing in the doorway. I wanted to walk over and apologise, to explain that she'd misread me. But I couldn't.

I wanted to tell her about the man with the roses.

Deedes ran at me. I shoved him away and he slipped, falling face first against the car. His nose began to pour blood. I was completely lost then. I ducked into the Fiesta, started the engine and pulled away. In the rear-view mirror, I could see Sue kneeling beside her fallen hero.

5

I drove around for a while, trying to think of somewhere to go; someone to visit who I could talk to. But there was no one. There never had been anyone – except Mother and Aunt Edna.

'Face it, Jem,' I told myself, 'you just don't know how to make friends.' It had been the same at school. Other people gathered in gangs while I kept to myself. I don't know where it began. I don't even know if there was a single point in time when little Jeremy Miller suddenly developed a talent for unpopularity. My pet theory used to be that I'd done something particularly dreadful in a previous existence. Now I wasn't sure.

I convinced myself that if I moved away from the area, I could take on a whole new identity. Fun-loving Jem, the life and soul of the party. So I joined a newspaper in Kent as a junior. Within three weeks, I'd annoyed the news editor, upset the chief reporter and got into needless arguments with two of my reporter colleagues. By the end of the first month it was business as usual for Jeremy Miller.

Jack the Lad.

Mr Flash.

Then I joined the *Herald*. I tried to play it low-key, but the mocking eyes and the viper tongue just wouldn't quit. In my third week, I asked Sue Cater out for a drink. She told me she was too busy.

'You're not too busy to brown-nose with Bateman every lunch hour,' I snapped. 'Or do you only drink with married men?'

'No, Jeremy,' she said icily. 'I only drink with men. Surly little boys are something of a turn-off.'

At that point, Bateman walked in. 'You fancy a drink, Sue?' he called from the door.

I leaned in to Sue. 'Sugar daddy's calling,' I whispered. Before she could reply, I turned on my heel and returned to my desk.

I could have written a degree course in stupidity.

I didn't sleep well that night. I sat stroking Chicken until well after 2 a.m., watching the rain beat against the grime of the window, forcing patterns into the dust. The kitten knew nothing of my distress. She curled herself into a contented ball and lay purring softly.

The following morning, I arrived at the office at 9.30 a.m. exactly. I didn't want to be early and have to sit in the silence I knew would surround me. As soon as I arrived, Thelma, the front-office receptionist, told me Don Bateman wanted to see me. I was expecting it and resolved not to start an argument.

The editor was away and Bateman was waiting in his sparsely furnished office on the second floor, next to the subs' room. He told me to sit down, which was not good news. The light was gleaming on Bateman's bald patch and throwing deep shadows around his flinty eyes.

'Last night was a disgrace,' he said, 'but that's not what this is about. It just brought things to a head. I don't mind you being a flash bastard, Miller. What I can't abide is the self-delusion you surround yourself with. You think you're a good reporter? Balls! You're not worth spit. Good reporters care about more than a pretty phrase or a nicely turned paragraph. Good reporters understand people. Your trouble, son, is that you talk a good story, but that's all it is: talk. Take this trick woman. Sounded fine – until I found out you hadn't even got her address. And then she wouldn't play ball. That's not quality. Why don't you give it up and go off somewhere to write poetry?'

'Are you sacking me?' I asked him.

'I wish I could.' He leaned back in his chair and lit a cigarette. 'There was a time, Jeremy, a golden time, when you could sack someone for being lousy at a job. But those times are long gone, thanks to the bastard socialists. Now it's all verbal warnings and written warnings. This, in case it hasn't filtered through, is a verbal warning.'

'I'm supposed to be allowed a representative of the union,' I said, before I could stop the words flowing.

He smiled. 'Yes, that's true. But Phil Deedes is Father of the Chapel and he's off sick, for some reason. Sue Cater is his assistant and she had an urgent appointment. Why don't you take my advice and quit?'

'If I did that it would still be constructive dismissal. I could sue.'

'So you could, son,' he said wearily.

'And don't call me "son",' I said, rising.

'I'm not finished yet, Miller. You promised a feature for page eight. Since your sprinting pensioner isn't available for comment, I want you to go and visit Dawn Green. Andrew has the details. We've plenty of file pictures.'

'Who's Dawn Green?'

'Ask Andrew. But be back by two, with copy presented by four.'

As I entered the reporters' room, I avoided looking at Sue Cater – who was clearly not at an urgent appointment – or any of the others. I had a feeling I'd been sent to Coventry and was determined to give no one the opportunity of snubbing me.

Andrew Evans waved me over. Andrew was the chief reporter. It wasn't an official title, exactly, since Don Bateman was already news editor, but he was accepted by all as Bateman's assistant and granted an honorary title. He was thirty-one years of age, tall and thin with sandy hair and pale blue eyes. Nostalgia tells me Andrew quite liked me, but in reality I think he just disliked me less than the others did. Then again, maybe that's just me being paranoid.

His desk was by the western window. There were six desks in the reporters' room, all with plywood screens at the front to give the illusion of privacy. Each workstation had its own telephone extension.

'Do you know about Dawn Green?' he asked. I shook my head. 'No? Okay. She lives up near Western Avenue, overlooking the dual carriageway. Lovely girl. She was injured in a car crash five years ago. She's twenty-six now. We carry stories periodically on how she's doing, but mainly we just make sure we pop in and see her every now and then. A bit of company. You understand?'

'I was told it's a feature for page eight.'

He shook his head. 'There's nothing new to say about Dawn.'

'Then what's the point of me going?'

He took a slow, deep breath. 'We all go, Jeremy. That's just the way it is. Most of us enjoy it. Some of us even go in our own time.'

'I'm not a hospital visitor.'

'I can well understand,' he said, very softly, 'how a rising superstar like yourself could find it offensive having to do the same things as the rest of us. But no one ever said life would be fair. Here's her address. She lives with her parents. Nice couple. Just introduce yourself and say we sent you. Stay about an hour.'

It was a pleasant spring morning and the sweetness of the sunlight even gave warmth to the grey stone of the old church. I drove east and found Dawn's house. I guess it was more of a large flat, really, since it was located above a newsagent's shop.

Mrs Green was behind the counter when I arrived, a bustling, middle-aged woman who greeted me like an old friend when I announced the purpose of my visit.

'Dawn will be so pleased,' she said. 'Just go up. Follow the stairs to the right.'

The room was small, her bed placed against the window. I say bed because that's where she was lying, but it was more of a contraption of knobs, wheels and levers.

In front of her face was a metal frame on which rested a book, held open by a steel stalk. A second stalk projected about an inch from a band around her forehead. As I stepped into the room, I saw her head move fractionally, tipping the stalk. Slowly, the page turned. At that moment, I wanted to turn and leave, but to do so would mean passing the mother at the shop counter. I cleared my throat.

'Who is it?'

She couldn't even turn her head.

'I'm Jeremy Miller, from the *Herald.*'

'Oh, hello. Isn't it a lovely day?'

'Beautiful.' I walked to the bedside and sat down in the chair that waited there. Now I could see her face. She wasn't lovely, as I'd feared, but somehow that made it worse. A beautiful crippled girl would have been as unreal as any Hollywood script, and I could have coped with that. But she was so … ordinary. Serene. How could she be anything else?

'How is everyone?' she asked.

'Who do you mean?'

'The rest of the staff.'

'All of them?'

She smiled. 'Yes. Tell me in alphabetical order.'

'You know Don Bateman?'

'Yes. Dear Don. I was so sorry when his marriage broke up. He's such a caring man. It must have hurt him terribly.'

'He was in fine fettle when I saw him this morning. *Very* caring.'

'Don't let him upset you. He only barks at people he likes.'

'Probably. I'm sorry, I know very little about you. What happened?'

Her eyes switched from my face to the ceiling. 'My fiancé and I were coming back from a party. I was asleep on the back seat. He crashed. I broke my neck.'

'Was he …? Did he …?'

'You *are* coy for a reporter.' Her eyes flicked back to me. 'No wonder Don barks at you. No, he didn't die. He wasn't hurt, thank goodness.'

'So where is he?'

'He lives in Ealing. He's got two children now, a boy and a girl. But what about you, Jeremy?'

'I thought you wanted to know about the staff.'

'Later. Tell me about Jeremy Miller, warts and all.'

'I don't have any warts. I'm true gold. Not a bad point in the entire repertoire. My mother thinks I ought to be canonised.'

'Are you married?'

'No. And no girlfriends, either. I'm saving myself for Sue Cater. Just waiting for the puddle across which I can throw my coat.'

30

She chuckled then. 'Have you asked her out yet?'

'Once. She declined. But I did give her a drink last night. Are you still getting hospital treatment?'

'For what? I'm a quadriplegic. There's no cure for that. I don't even think about it any more. This is my life, and it's really very good. I have lots of friends who come to see me. Mummy talks about Lourdes, but it doesn't strike me as a very good idea. I don't need Lourdes to be happy. I don't need legs or arms. I have friends, and I have books. And I see people every day from my window.'

'And you're not bitter?'

'I dealt with that years ago, Jeremy. If you're lucky, like I am, you go past the "Why me?" and ask, "Why not me?" That's where you find answers.'

'Are you religious?'

'Are you?' she countered.

'No. My mother is, ever since my father died. She needs to believe he's still there somewhere. Close by. Still loving her as he always did. She talks to him. Mostly in the garden – it's where we scattered his ashes.'

'Maybe she's right,' said Dawn. 'Maybe he is there.'

'That would be nice.'

For the next hour, we talked of life, love, cats, books, films and journalism. Somewhere during that hour, I produced my notebook and filled page after page with Pitman shorthand. One quote still remains in my mind. We spoke of the view from the window and how, the night before, she'd watched a youth walk along a line of cars, scoring the paint with a penknife.

'I felt so sorry for him. He must be very unhappy. He looked up and saw my face at the window and he raised two fingers at me. All I could do was smile, because that's all

God's left me with. But I wouldn't swap lives with that boy even if I could.'

'Not even to walk again?'

'Not at the risk of experiencing his anger, hatred and bitterness. I don't need the strength to raise two fingers at the world. That's the nicest thing, really. When a smile is all you have, you find it really is all you need.'

If anyone else had said that, I'd have cracked up. It should have sounded like a quote from a Disney cartoon character just before it burst into some wet song. But it didn't. And I didn't laugh.

'I'll come and see you again soon,' I told her.

'I wasn't too boring, was I?'

'Are you kidding? I've had a great time.'

Outside in the sunlight once more, I found myself feeling strangely rested. All around me there were people hurrying by. I saw them differently now, although I realised it would be a short-lived empathy. I looked up and saw her face in the window, and answered her smile with one of my own.

Back at the office, I began to type furiously, desperate to convey the emotions she had inspired in me, and the sense of joy felt by the girl in the window. Most of all, I wanted it to be read by the youth with the penknife. Don Bateman checked the feature and said it wasn't bad. John French, the chief sub, designed the page with two stock pictures and a new one, taken from the street.

The headline running across the seven-column page read THE FACE IN THE WINDOW. Underneath it, John had placed a sentence from the article, which I'd part-borrowed from a Meryl Streep movie: *Looking at the world through the eyes of God.*

I was very pleased with the piece.

So was Ethel Hurst. Obviously her disavowal of modern

papers didn't mean she had stopped reading them. She rang me on Friday morning to say it had made her cry. And she invited me for tea.

6

The front page of the paper was mostly taken up by the murder. The grisliest of the facts had been excluded from the report, which merely said that divorcee Mrs Barbara Sinclair had been savagely murdered in her home in the early hours of Tuesday morning. After that it was details of her life, quotes from shocked neighbours and a police spokesman saying it was 'one of the most brutal crimes I have ever witnessed.' I wondered at the time if policemen carried little books of adequate quotations to cover any eventuality. Or should that be inadequate quotations?

Whatever. Phil Deedes had managed to dig up a photo of Mrs Sinclair, who was now to be seen beaming from the front page. The contrast was quite chilling. A smiling woman surrounded by words describing her death.

Ethel Hurst was most distressed by the case. 'You can tell she was a nice woman,' she said as she poured tea. 'Not so much by the photograph, but by the comments of her friends.'

It felt unwise to point out that people rarely spoke ill of the dead.

'I'm sure I've seen her at Tesco's, shopping,' said Ethel. 'Terrible that there are people living among us who seem to enjoy inflicting pain.'

'There have been people like that since before the Vikings, Mrs Hurst. Are you reconsidering doing my article?'

'Goodness, no!' she said. She leaned back in her white vinyl armchair and tucked a rogue strand of hair behind her ear. 'But among other things, I wanted to tell you how sensitive I felt your story was about poor Dawn Green. I was moved to tears. I wanted to know more about her.'

'I'm not sure what else I can tell you. She's happy. I don't know why. She said it herself. There's no anger, no bitterness. She sees every day as a joy.'

'Which it is!' said Ethel. 'Or rather, how it ought to be. Every morning, as I awake, I say a prayer of thanks to the Almighty for the privilege of watching the sun rise and set.'

'So you believe in God?'

'How could I not? Have you ever smelled a Red Velvet rose? Nothing so beautiful could ever happen by chance.'

I smiled and nodded. My first sexual encounter had been in the back of an Escort van on a grubby blanket, groping a woman I'd only just met. That had been beautiful, too, even if I didn't get her knickers off, but it hadn't convinced me God was in his Heaven. 'Jesus Christ, you've ripped my dress!' was hardly Damascus Road material.

I finished my tea and thanked her, reaching for my coat.

'Oh, don't go yet,' she said. 'I still have to ask your advice.'

'About what?'

'About the murder. I was wondering if the police would consider it an impertinence if I offered to help.'

Don Bateman was right. I wasn't worth spit. Here was a woman who appeared to have real psychic power. To link her with the murder case would be front-page news.

'What would you do?' I asked her.

'Well, if the dead woman had a gold or silver ring, I could probably say how she died and who killed her.'

A dark shadow fell across me and I jumped. Towering

beside me was the awesome Sutcliffe. I felt again that un-natural fear.

'Not wise, Mrs Hurst,' he said, his voice deep and rolling.

'Mr Sutcliffe has many powers,' said Ethel, 'in addition to his brilliance with my roses. He feels I may be in personal danger if I involve myself. Do you think that's the case, Mr Miller?'

I let the question free-fall through my thoughts. 'I wouldn't think so. If you can identify the man, the police will arrest him right away if they believe you. If you can't, then you're no danger to him.'

'My thoughts exactly. Mr Sutcliffe thinks he will strike again. I want to stop that happening.'

'That cannot be done,' said Sutcliffe, 'but perhaps you should try after all. I will see you later, Mrs Hurst.'

After he'd gone, my shoulders sagged into relaxation once more. Ethel noticed my relief.

'He is a strange man, but he is my friend. Your generation often mistake the word, taking it to mean a drinking com-panion, or a work colleague. It is more than that. It is like finding a brother or sister you never knew existed. It is a kind of love, Mr Miller. You need have no fear of Mr Sutcliffe.'

'That's nice to know. But for some reason I find his pres-ence unsettling.'

Ethel leaned forward and touched the teapot. Finding it still hot, she poured us both fresh cups. 'He unsettles you because you are a Sensitive. That is, a latent psychic. And you can feel in your soul that he has killed people. Sugar?'

It ranked as one of the greatest conversation-stoppers I had ever encountered. A gentle-eyed old lady was pouring tea into fine bone china cups, in the midst of a room fes-tooned with delicate glass figures, while casually mention-ing that I had no need to fear a man who had killed before.

I sipped the blended Earl Grey tea. 'Would you mind explaining that to me, Mrs Hurst?'

'About you being a latent psychic?'

'No. About Mr Sutcliffe killing people. I take it that isn't a hobby?'

She smiled and tilted her head. 'You should try to relax more, Jeremy. Call me Ethel. And you must remember, dear, that Mr Sutcliffe is, like me, no longer young. In fact, though he doesn't look it, he is almost seventy.' That surprised me almost more than his violent past. The man looked no more than middle-aged, and immensely powerful. 'He is from Rhodesia,' said Ethel. 'I understand his mother was Zulu and his father Matabele. They're tribes, you know?'

'I've seen the movie.'

'I'm sorry?'

'There was a film with Stanley Baker. I believe the Zulus were mentioned. It doesn't matter.'

'Oh, I see. Mr Sutcliffe was born near Bulawayo towards the end of the First World War. His father was quite wealthy, by his own lights, owning many cattle and goats. There was also some money from land they sold to a mining company. Anyway, Mr Sutcliffe received schooling far in advance of many of his contemporaries. He was, and is, a very intelligent man, and at the start of the Second World War, he enlisted. He fought in Europe and Burma – he was a sniper, I believe. After the war, he returned home. He doesn't talk much about those times, but he was deeply distressed by some of the events in that area and joined Joshua Nkomo. For many years, Mr Sutcliffe was a partisan. He even went to Russia at some stage. He speaks a little Russian – wonderful language, so expressive. When Rhodesia finally became Zimbabwe, he left to settle in England. I think that's about it.'

I placed my cup on the glass-topped table. 'I don't think that can be it, Ethel. Firstly, Mr Sutcliffe is the most unusual Zulu name I've come across. Secondly, if he spent his latter years trying to free Rhodesia, what's he doing in Britain now? Why isn't he enjoying the fruits of his triumphs in Harare?'

'Those are questions for Mr Sutcliffe.' It was as if an invisible wall had come down between us. I think Ethel had expected a different response from me, but I couldn't grasp the gossamer line she was willing me to take.

'How did you meet him?' I asked, in an effort to gain time.

'I met him in Cairo. I was with an old friend and we were attacked in the street. Mr Sutcliffe frightened the criminals away and bought us tea.'

'I'm very tempted to stop asking questions,' I said with a smile. 'Every answer just opens fresh avenues. Cairo?'

'It was a holiday. I wanted to see the Sphinx and the Great Pyramid of Cheops.'

'And while you were there, you were rescued by a giant Zulu terrorist who followed you to England to put up your bookshelves?'

She chuckled. 'It is difficult to condense so many years into a brief outline. Firstly, he is not Zulu, but Matabele. Secondly, he did not follow me to England. After he saw us back to our hotel in Cairo, he said goodbye. We didn't meet again until twelve years later. It was at Wimbledon in 1983. I can't remember who won. I suppose it was Miss Navratilova. Anyway, I was just leaving the stands when I saw this huge figure. I felt sure it was him but couldn't believe it. I walked up behind him, and he turned and smiled. "How are you, Mrs Hurst?" he said, almost before he'd seen me. It was quite a shock.'

'And then you became friends?'

'Yes. We had tea in a small café. You should have seen the looks we got.'

'I can imagine. Why does he still call you Mrs Hurst? Why not Ethel?'

For the first time, she looked embarrassed, a delicate pink appearing on her cheeks. 'I am sixty-four years of age, Jeremy. Mr Sutcliffe is sixty-nine. He felt there should be a boundary to our friendship. The line is drawn at mutual respect.'

'But you said earlier that it's a kind of love?'

'That is what friendship is. We are not lovers. Nor have we ever been. But in some ways we are closer than that.'

'Will he be angry at you for telling me all this?'

'Goodness, no. He insisted on it.'

'Why?'

'Because he says you can be trusted not to betray him – or me.'

'I'm afraid this is all drifting by me like smoke. He doesn't know me. You don't know me.'

'Mr Sutcliffe doesn't need to know you, in the sense of learning someone's life story. He is a man of the earth. His senses are acute. When he says you can be trusted, then that is how it is. Now, what do we do about helping the police?'

'I don't think it's going to be quite that easy. Policemen are pragmatic people. They believe in nothing they can't see. We'll have to be very convincing. How certain is this power of yours?'

'In what way "certain"?'

'Is it always there when you need it?'

'No, not always.'

'Wonderful. You're going to be sitting at the centre of a sea of scepticism. I hope you're prepared to be a laughing stock.'

'I am far too long in the tooth to be concerned about ego. Set it up for me, Jeremy. I'm sure the police will listen to you.'

It wasn't the police I was worried about as I returned to the office. It was Don Bateman.

As I pushed open the front door, Oliver Cappel was on his way out. He was the junior reporter, taken on in the autumn. 'How's it going?' I said. He walked past me as if I didn't exist.

I found Bateman sitting with John French discussing centre-page layouts for the following week's paper. 'Could I have a word with you?' I asked.

'Come back in ten minutes,' answered Bateman, without looking up. Anger welled inside me but I bit it back. On the top floor, Andrew Evans and Sue Cater were sitting together, enjoying a coffee. Phil Deedes was typing. No one spoke as I entered. I tidied my desk for several minutes then moved to the sink and switched on the electric kettle. It was then that I saw my mug was broken. It had been a gift from my mother, a simple blue coffee mug with the words *Silent: Genius at Work* on the side. It was now in four pieces. Oliver Cappel's blue and white QPR mug was clean so I made myself a coffee in that and returned to my seat. The conversation between Sue and Andrew was now sounding unnaturally loud, almost strident, as if I were witnessing a play from a seat too close to the stage. I leaned back and lifted my feet onto the desk. I desperately wanted to apologise to Sue and yet was prevented, not by simple pride, but by a stubborn refusal to submit to the tactics employed by my colleagues. I knew what I'd done was wrong, but if I apologised, I feared it would look as if they had cowed me. I was trapped, and unhappy.

Cappel appeared at my desk. 'You're using my mug,' he said.

I swung my legs down and stood. He was a short, spotty boy who would be bald by the age of twenty-five.

'You don't understand this "Coventry" business, Oliver,' I said. 'The object is to not speak to the victim. To treat him as if he isn't there. Now, if you don't mind a little advice, you should have just walked up and taken the cup without a word, thus signalling your contempt.'

'Maybe I thought you'd throw its contents over me,' he snapped.

'I'd be unlikely to do anything that might improve your looks. And let's face it, even a mask of coffee would be better than staring at your festering sores.' I drained the coffee and offered him the cup, but he just walked away, his face a deep, beetroot red, offset by the white-topped spots on his chin.

As the door closed behind him, a raw, angry silence enveloped me. It was broken after several seconds by Andrew Evans.

'You really can be a dreadful shit, Jeremy,' he said, in his normal neutral voice.

'I can be worse than that, Andrew. If you pricks want to play silly games, you should make sure all the players know the rules. And, for the record, I am sorry that I wet the pompous cow. And I'm equally sorry that Rambo there tripped and hurt his nose. But I'm not taking crap from the likes of any of you dead-heads.'

'Your graceful apology is noted,' said Andrew. 'But bear this in mind: you've a considerable way to climb before you're fit to lace the shoes of the "dead-heads" here. Even Oliver works harder than you do.'

All I could do was nod. No one likes being wrong, and I had just dug my pit ever deeper.

With the ten minutes gone, I located Don Bateman in the

editor's office, and once again we faced each other across the desk. I outlined Ethel's offer, and he listened in grim silence.

'She's not a trickster? You're sure of that?'

'I'm pretty sure.'

'I'll speak to Ray, but I don't think he'll buy it.' Ray was Superintendent Ray Morris, a hard northerner who'd been in the town for six years. 'On the other hand,' he mused, 'the police psychologist reckons there's a good chance the killer will strike again. I don't know … Come back at five.'

'It's a great story, though, isn't it? Psychic helps police in killer hunt.'

'I won't deny that,' said Bateman. 'How did you talk her into it?'

'Just talent, I guess,' I said, moving to the door. I stopped and turned. 'No, it wasn't talent. She read my Dawn Green piece and invited me for tea. It was all her idea. It hadn't even occurred to me.'

He nodded. 'That Dawn piece was fine. Very fine. That was a superb line about looking at the world through the eyes of God.'

Still gripped by the spirit of confession, I told him it was from a movie.

'I know – *Out of Africa* with Meryl Streep.'

I went back to my typewriter and completed my stories. Andrew Evans was right. I was a slacker. But not any more, I decided. I lost track of time and it was 6.20 p.m. when Don Bateman came and found me working alone in the reporters' room.

'Ray Morris is willing to see your woman at ten a.m. tomorrow. But there's to be no publicity. If she turns out to be helpful, we can print the story following a conviction.'

'Then we get nothing?'

'If you're right, we may get a killer and save some lives. Isn't that enough?'

'It's enough for Ethel and Mr Sutcliffe.'

'Sutcliffe?'

I realised I hadn't mentioned the giant.

'Just someone else from *Out of Africa*,' I told him.

7

All in all, this had been a good day, he thought as he left the late-night cinema. Marry had been in a good mood, and they'd spent the morning laughing together, trying to make some sense of the chaos that was their garden. They planted two new rose bushes, double gifts to celebrate the love they felt for one another. He had chosen Silver Jubilee, in the hope they would have a quarter of a century together. Marry had selected Apache. They had planted them too close together, but, in the spirit of romance, they wanted the branches to interweave.

Marry was working tonight and so he'd gone to the cinema, where they were showing a series of Jack Nicholson films concluding with *Terms of Endearment*. He cried at the end. Sad films affected him like that. The dying mother trying to find the words to say farewell to her young son had caused his throat to swell, his eyes to burn. There weren't many people in the cinema, which he felt was a shame. There was so much to be learned from such a quality film.

It was 1 a.m. when the blue Sierra pulled into Madeira Drive. He parked it under an overhanging tree at the corner and removed his jacket. It was a warm night and the stars overhead swirled around the moon like magic dust. He recalled his disappointment in 1969 when the Americans had landed on the moon. Some things were too beautiful to be sullied.

He walked through the alleyway separating Madeira Drive from Sunley Close and waited at the corner, staring at the silent houses. He remembered his father saying once that windows represented the eyes of houses. When the lights were out, the houses were asleep; but when they came on, the buildings sat like great monsters staring into the street. All the houses in Sunley Close were asleep.

He walked to number twenty-three and along the side of the house to the back garden.

It was such a lovely night. Sweat dripped into his eyes and he mopped his brow with a white linen handkerchief. The back door was locked, but a small window had been left open beside the kitchen. He hooked his arm inside and opened the main window, then climbed in over the sink and down to the floor beside the refrigerator. His heart was beating fast now and fear was filling his blood with adrenaline. He wanted to leave. He wanted to run to the car. But he couldn't. It had all gone too far now. Removing his gloves, he fished into the deep thigh pockets of the dyed-black military trousers and produced the items he would need.

Upstairs, Mrs Dorothy Bowyer dreamed of golden sands and a deep, blue sea.

8

I was with Ethel on Saturday morning when the phone rang at 9.15 a.m. Ray Morris couldn't make the 10 a.m. meeting but would see her at noon, if that was convenient. She said that it was. I phoned Don Bateman to ask whether I should return to the office, but he told me to stay with Ethel and gather background information.

For some reason, I felt more nervous than she did, rather like an impresario waiting for his novice singer to walk onstage before the first-night audience. Ethel appeared unaffected. She was wearing a pleated pink skirt and a simple white cotton blouse adorned with a silver filigree butterfly. She looked like grandmothers are supposed to look, sweet and wholesome, and possessed of an infinite kindness. She made me some toast and told me stories about her husband Freddie; about his absent-mindedness, and his gentle sense of humour. He sounded like a pleasant man. He had died of a heart attack in his sleep. I couldn't imagine anything worse than waking up next to a corpse, but Ethel had taken it to be a gift from Heaven.

'Freddie was so happy that day. He'd been to a reunion of his army chums and drunk a little too much beer. I cooked him a fried egg sandwich at midnight, and then he went to bed. He wasn't a man who showed his feelings much. He didn't like to hold hands in public, that sort of thing. But that night, he leaned over and kissed me goodnight. It was probably the drink. And he said, "Thank you." Just that. He looked into my eyes and he thanked me. It was terribly sweet. But, you know, it makes for a wonderful memory. I'll get you some more tea.'

If I'd been older then, or more assured, I might have followed Ethel into the kitchen and just put my arms around her. I could see by the brightness of her eyes that the memory distressed her. But, as usual, I sat cursing the walls of my tower. Somewhere deep in the tangled insecurity of adolescence, I'd built it to keep hurt from me. Unfortunately, from the outside, its walls were paper and anyone could enter. But if I tried to leave, it was granite. More a prison than a fortress.

When she returned, I could see she was still upset, so I asked about her early life.

She had been born in the borough to a family of four. Her father, Frank Osborne, had lost a leg in the First World War and died of tuberculosis in 1925. Her mother, Elizabeth, passed away ten years later. Ethel was raised by an older sister called Florence. There was another sister, May, and a brother, Alfred. Florence suffered a stroke in 1951 and died a year later, having never recovered the power of speech. Alfred was killed in the desert during World War Two, while May had fallen foul of cancer two years ago. Now Ethel alone remained, the last of the Osborne line. She seemed to bear the burden heavily.

We arrived at the police station at 11.45 a.m. and the station sergeant took us to the canteen. There we were given yet more tea until 11.55, when we were ushered into Ray Morris's large office on the top floor. Don Bateman was already there, along with Chief Inspector Frank Beard and a CID officer I'd met before but whose name I couldn't recall. There were no introductions. The CID man looked bored and faintly uneasy, while Frank Beard wore his scepticism like a rosette.

Ray Morris stood as we entered and moved around the imposing desk to shake hands with Ethel.

'It's good of you to offer to help, Mrs Hurst,' he said, smiling. 'I hope you won't find this a waste of your valuable time.'

I couldn't tell if there was sarcasm hidden in those heavy northern vowels. Back then, I believed northern wit had all the subtle flavour of a brick sandwich. Now I am not so sure.

'Not at all, Superintendent,' said Ethel.

Morris showed her to a chair in front of the desk and she sat, removing her white gloves and placing them neatly on the desktop alongside three plastic envelopes. Two contained golden rings, the third a brooch in the shape of a coiled snake. Morris sat himself opposite Ethel.

'I hope you won't be offended, Mrs Hurst, but two of the objects before you were not owned by the murdered woman.'

'I'm not offended,' said Ethel. 'I am sure it is very wise of you. May I remove them from the envelopes?' He nodded. Ethel selected the ring on the left, slipping her index finger inside the plastic bag, but didn't take out the band. She moved to the next ring. As her finger touched it, she jerked.

'Could I have a little water?' she asked.

Morris glanced up at the CID man, who brought her a glass. She sipped it slowly, and I noticed then the gleam of perspiration on her brow. She took a deep breath and, with a sudden movement, tipped the ring onto her palm, closing her fingers around it.

'There is a room,' she said, her voice trembling. 'Dark furniture. A painting on the wall showing a yacht on a lake. The door is opening. I am asleep. I hear a noise and I wake. A dark shadow is looming. The face is black ... No! Not a face, a mask. The word "Death" is embroidered across the brow. I can't move. I can't scream. He doesn't speak. He grabs my arm and forces me to turn onto my stomach. Something cold touches the back of my neck.'

She groaned and swayed in the chair. I reached out in case she fell. She said nothing for several minutes, then her eyes opened and she looked straight at Ray Morris.

'This is why you delayed our meeting?' she asked.

He nodded.

'What's happening, Ray?' asked Bateman.

'You tell him, Mrs Hurst.'

'There has been a second murder. I believe her name was Bowyer,' said Ethel.

Bateman looked at Morris, who nodded. The CID man was no longer bored.

'Describe the man again,' he said, moving closer and opening his notebook. I remembered him then – Detective Sergeant Adams.

'He is over six feet tall and strongly built. He wears black leather gloves and a balaclava-type hooded mask. The word "Death" is embroidered in white. Delicately embroidered. His eyes are blue. He used a needle and thread to ... I can't!' She fell silent and sipped the water once more.

'Would you like something a little stronger, Mrs Hurst?' asked Frank Beard, his scepticism vanished.

'No thank you, Mr Beard. And don't forget to collect your wife's wedding ring,' she said, pointing at the first envelope.

'Did you see the weapon he used?' asked Adams.

'Yes. It was an upholstery needle wedged into a cork. He had to remove it with a small pair of pliers.'

'You can't get inside his mind?'

'Not fully. I would need something of his to do that. But I sense both triumph and fear, and a terrible confusion.'

'Confusion?' said Adams.

'I can't explain it. It's as if the woman had two faces. Do you understand?'

Adams shook his head.

Ethel took a deep breath. 'I think he was seeing another face as he killed her. That's all I can tell you about him.'

'What about the rest of his clothes?' queried Beard.

'He wore a dark – possibly black – sweater and dark trousers. Like the ones you see in the army films, with large pockets on the outside of the thighs. His shoes were like those used by runners. They were grey.' She picked up the ring again. 'Yes, there are two words on the shoes – Hi-Tec. Is that helpful?'

'One of the cheapest and most popular brands on the market,' I said.

'Do you feel up to examining the brooch, Mrs Hurst?' said Morris. 'It belonged to Mrs Sinclair, the first victim. She had no rings.'

'I don't think I can today, Mr Morris. I'm awfully sorry but I feel a little ill. Why did he stitch her together like that?'

'I wish we knew,' Morris replied. 'Tell me something – when you held the ring, you spoke as if you were Mrs Bowyer. Can you see any link between the victims?'

'Oh, I can tell you that,' said Ethel. 'Dorothy … yes, that was her name … was terrified at the moment of her death. She was thinking about the woman killed last week. She did not know her. She couldn't even remember the first victim's name.'

'Can Detective Sergeant Adams here visit you tomorrow?'

'Yes, of course. I'm sorry to be such a nuisance. I don't have a very strong stomach.'

Don Bateman stood and signalled for me to join him. 'Take Mrs Hurst to the canteen. Give her some sweet tea – she looks in shock. I'll see you there in a bit.'

A short while later, as we sat together nursing plastic cups of truly dreadful tea, Ethel took my hand. 'I wasn't much help, Jeremy. And it was all so dreadful.'

'You were fine,' I assured her.

'Mr Sutcliffe says we're now part of the evil. He says it's a circle that will slowly close around us. I don't want to be killed like that, Jeremy.'

'No one will know you're helping us, I promise you.' I wanted to tell her I didn't believe in such psychic bullshit, but it's hard to find the words when you've just witnessed an elderly lady apparently linking minds with a murder victim.

'You will be careful, won't you?' she said.

'Careful of what?'

She sighed. 'I don't really know.'

As the office door closed behind Jeremy and Mrs Hurst, Don Bateman moved to the chair facing Ray Morris.

'You don't have to tell me how right she was. I could see it in your faces.'

'Not a word of this in print, Don,' said Morris.

'I don't need to give my word more than once,' said Bateman, 'but you can't keep this story down for long, either, and I won't risk someone else carrying it before we do. There's another bastard Yorkshire Ripper out there. How long does it stay under wraps?'

Morris shrugged. 'Give me another three days.'

'Too long.'

'Jesus, Don! You're a weekly, for goodness sake. Three days is fine for your deadlines.'

'Maybe, but I'm also a stringer for the *Mirror*. Puts a few more crusts on the table. Now, I agreed to say nothing about the psychic. I did *not* agree to keep a second killing quiet.'

'I'm not asking for quiet, Don. I'm asking for *nothing* to be said about hooded masks embroidered with the word "Death". And I don't want Yorkshire Ripper headlines, either.'

Bateman shook his head and smiled. 'You can't stop them, Ray. I know enough about policework to know that most killings are family affairs – disgruntled husbands, ex-boyfriends, jealous wives. The real tough nuts to crack are the motiveless murders, the cranks and the weirdos. You think this one's going to be satisfied with two?'

Morris shrugged. 'There could still be a link. It doesn't have to be a headcase.'

Bateman nodded sympathetically. Morris was clutching at straws.

'What do forensics show?'

'Off the record?'

'For now. I'll come back to you for the quotes tomorrow.'

'Okay.' Morris opened a green folder. 'Nothing unusual about the semen found inside Mrs Sinclair. Marginally subfertile, maybe suggesting a man over forty. Some black fibres were found in her pubic hair and our lab guy reckons they were from a woollen sweater. There was also a tiny white fibre which he initially thought might be from a scarf. It now looks like it was from the embroidered balaclava. Cause of death was a long, thin needle driven up into the base of her skull.'

'What about the stitching?'

'Neat, but not expert. Black thread and a curved needle, possibly surgical.'

'And Mrs Bowyer?' asked Bateman.

'Still waiting for the lab, but I'd bet a pound to a bent

penny the MO is the same. There was a trickle of blood on the back of her neck. And she'd been stitched.'

'What do you know about her?'

'Telephonist. Aged forty-one. Divorced, no children. Local girl.'

'What about the ex-husbands?'

'This is still off the record, Don, OK? Sinclair's ex is a personnel manager at Watkins Industrial. They split up three years ago. She had several affairs. He used to knock her about – he admits that – but the night she was murdered, he was at a conference in Holland. And you can forget faked passports, secret trips home and all that *Sweeney* crap. He was taken ill with suspected food poisoning and spent two nights in hospital under supervision.'

'And Mrs Bowyer's ex?'

'Physical training instructor at the local school. They split up eight years ago, when he had an affair with another teacher. They're now married, three kids. He used to take his ex-wife out once a week. They stayed friends.'

'I don't relish your job, Ray,' said Bateman. 'I think you're going to need a lot of luck.'

'Mrs Hurst is a start,' said Morris. 'That was uncanny. How come we've never heard of her before?'

'No idea. Young Miller's been trying to get a feature out of her. She refused. Next thing, she's offering to help solve the murder. Nice old bird, though. I don't think she's publicity hunting.'

'Neither do I. But you'd better keep her name quiet, all the same. I don't want the killer paying her a visit.'

'Good point. Before I go, who tipped you off about the Bowyer woman?'

'Anonymous call to the front desk. A man.'

'Same as before?'

'Hard to say. Different officer on duty. We've a tape on it now for all calls.'

'Okay. Thanks for your time, lads. And just so we're clear, no one speaks to Mrs Hurst unless a reporter is present. This is our story, and we want everything for when we can run it. If they do, all bets are off.'

'Understood, Don. But play down the headlines, will you? We don't want panic.'

9

The following morning proved to be an anticlimax when Ethel failed to 'read' anything of value from the coiled-snake brooch. As she explained to a disappointed Detective Sergeant Adams, the brooch wasn't worn next to the skin, and although she could tell it had been bought in Truro during a summer holiday eleven years ago, it was no help in solving the crime.

Ethel was very downcast after Adams had departed. She cleared away the teacups and replaced the lid on the brass biscuit barrel, then moved about the room idly lifting and rearranging the glass animals on the mantel shelf.

'It's early days,' I said. 'And you've already given the police a lot of help.'

'In what way?' she whispered, sitting down and facing me.

'They now know it was a tall man, broad-shouldered, wearing dark-coloured fatigues. They didn't know any of that before.'

'It's not a lot, though, is it? I had hoped to see his face and then pick him out from the mug shots.'

I chuckled. Somehow Ethel was not the right person to use the term 'mug shots'. It was like finding Clint Eastwood knitting baby booties. Ethel smiled, and I could see the tension easing from her.

'*Hill Street Blues*,' she said. 'Do you watch it?' I shook my head. I was no television fan. 'It's a wonderful programme about policemen in America. Oh dear, Jeremy, what can we do about this awful person?'

'They'll catch him, Ethel. They'll find more clues. You'll see.'

'I know that. But where will they find them? Mr Sutcliffe was right – there will be more brutality. Yesterday was quite dreadful. She was so frightened.'

'What else does Mr Sutcliffe think?'

'He says there will be other victims. He says they are already chosen.'

'How does he know?'

'I told you before, he is a man of the earth. He is a seer.'

I stayed with Ethel for another hour, then took the rest of the day off. On Monday I reported back to the office. I worked on two stories and made three contact calls during the afternoon to pick up paragraphs for our 'news in brief' columns. Bateman summoned me just after 4 p.m.

'Phil Deedes is stuck in County Court and we've had a call from one of the ex-husbands. It seems he's now ready to talk to us. Gary Sinclair, the personnel man. Get out to his house and gather some background. Jerry will meet you there for a picture.' He gave me the address, which turned out to be a semi-detached house in a quiet cul-de-sac in the east of town. There was a white Ford XR 3i parked outside.

I rang the bell and the door opened even before my finger had stopped pressing. Gary Sinclair looked tired. His eyes were dull, his smile weary.

'The *Herald*, right?'

'Yes, Jeremy Miller.' He stepped aside and I moved into the narrow hallway and through to a long lounge. There was an ox-hide rug set before a Chesterfield sofa and two dimpled leather armchairs. I sat down in a chair and pulled my notebook clear of my coat pocket, placed it on the floor and leaned back. He seemed to relax then. It's always wise not to go straight into questions. People are understandably nervous when faced with reporters.

'Would you like a coffee?' he asked. I nodded, smiled and thanked him. In his absence, I scanned the room, seeking to learn something about the man. It was tidy and tastefully decorated. There were two oil paintings on the pine-panelled walls, both landscapes. I moved to the book-shelf by the French windows. Thrillers, encyclopaedias, biographies of Muhammed Ali and Oscar Wilde, a couple of Dorothy Dunnett historical sagas.

'How do you like your coffee?' Gary called from the kitchen.

'White with two, thanks.'

I returned to the chair just as Gary returned with my drink. The coffee was strong and rich. I think he said it was Blue Mountain blended with Old Java. He bought it at a small shop in Richmond. After a while, I picked up my notebook.

'I understand you and Barbara were divorced three years ago?'

'No, that's when we separated. Nine years of purgatory we had together. I don't know whether I should be saying this. Everyone speaks so highly of her now she's dead, but she was a real cow. I can't remember her ever doing anything that wasn't selfish. Even when she helped people out, it was only so she could brag about how nice she was.'

He ran his hand through his hair and grinned self-consciously. 'I was in hospital when my boss came to me with the news. He sat down on the bed, with this sombre expression on his face, and said, "There's been a dreadful accident." Then he told me that Barbara had been found dead. That was all we knew then.'

'How did you feel?'

'Numb. It wasn't real. Lying in a hospital bed in Amsterdam, staring out at an alien city.' His eyes were no longer dull. They locked on to mine. 'I loved her. Very much. I loved her even when she lied. Even when she cheated. I even loved her the day I beat her up. I'm not a violent man, Mr Miller, but I broke her cheekbone and she was in hospital for six days. That's when I left her.' He stood and moved to the painting above the gas fire, staring into the glass-covered canvas horizon. 'She always dreamed of finding her perfect love, and she equated love with sex. If a man gave her an orgasm, he was finished. I think she spent her life waiting for the earth to move. She'd fall in love with blistering speed and then blame the man a couple of months later for not being the One.' He turned back to me. 'Do you understand what I'm saying?'

'Not really. She slept around?'

'No. I could have accepted that. She needed to be in love. All the time. She wanted a man to adore, and who would adore her. She saw life like a thirties movie. No man who adored her would complain about her spending, or grumble if the sheets weren't changed. The impossible dream. She thought ... Who knows what she thought? Whatever it was, it left her unhappy and unfulfilled. In turn, she made life hell for people who did love her. Because they could never love her enough.'

'You think she might have known the man who killed her?'

'You can bet on it,' said Sinclair.

After that, I gathered general background – how they met, where they married – and headed off. The photographer, Jerry Lewis, arrived as I was leaving. He didn't speak to me.

I went back to the now-empty office and typed up my notes, composing a short piece about the grieving ex-husband. When I'd finished, I leaned back and looked around. Cappel's desk was untidy. Sue Cater's was clean, the pencils in a neat line. The anger was gone now from the office, the atmosphere silently neutral, unlike during the day. I was forced to admit that the hostility was beginning to unnerve me. It was curious how I had never grown used to being unpopular. As a small child, I felt compelled to stand apart when other children played. I would watch them from behind walls. As a schoolboy, I had no friends, and at college only petty enemies. Yet here at the *Herald*, where no one knew me, I had thought to make a fresh start.

'I actually like you all,' I said, the words hanging in the air. 'And if you knew me – *really* knew me – you'd like me, too.'

Back home, I fed the cats and settled down for a quiet evening with Radio Four.

Nursing a half-tumbler of scotch with a dash of lemonade, I lay back on my sofa and listened to the report of the day's dealings in Parliament. Everyone sounded so serious, as if their words and deeds were of genuine importance. One of the few points of agreement I'd found with Don Bateman was when he said, 'You can always tell when a politician is lying: his lips move.'

I interviewed a psychiatrist once. He gave me some alarming information. He said there were thirty-five accepted tests to establish normality – or, if you like, sanity. But anyone who passed all thirty-five would be unusual, and therefore not normal. Heads you win, tails you lose. He also added that the normal person desires little more than a pleasant home, a loving family and good health. Only the abnormal have a desire to govern others. Only someone very abnormal wants to govern everybody.

Therefore, by definition, all presidents and prime ministers are headcases.

He didn't actually say that. That was my precis of his words. I stand by them.

I switched the radio to stereo cassette and inserted a Bob Dylan album. Rain was tapping at my window, I was mildly drunk and very lonely, and Dylan felt like just the right companion. Actually, that's not true. Sue Cater would have been the right companion. Not the lofty Sue I worked with, but the Sue of my fantasies, the soft, warm woman who would stroke away my tensions and kiss away my burdens.

It was around this point that the doorbell rang. For several delicious seconds, I allowed myself to think it might be her. I knew it wasn't.

I realised how drunk I was when I had to grip the banister on my way downstairs. I opened the door to see the giant Sutcliffe standing on the porch, rain gleaming on his jet-black face and dripping from his greying beard. He stepped inside without a greeting and moved up the stairs.

'Do come in,' I told his retreating back. When I arrived in my own flat, I found him divested of his dripping coat and sitting on the sofa with Rascal and Chicken both in his lap. Piddler was beside him, her head on his leg.

'Drink?' I asked.

'Coffee,' he answered. 'Black.'

'You like cats?'

'Yes. They taste very much like chicken.' The trace of humour in those dark eyes was fleeting. I could barely tell it was there. I made the coffee and sat down opposite him. It was almost 10 p.m., late for a social call. Yet he sat and drank his coffee in silence, idly stroking the cats, who lay and purred shamelessly in this stranger's lap.

'They know me better than you do,' he said.

'To know you is to love you, Mr Sutcliffe.'

'I see the drink has relaxed you, Jeremy. That is good. If

you learn to do it without the drink, that would be better.'

'I'm sure you didn't come here to advise me on my diet.'

'No. I am here to talk of Mrs Hurst. She is a very special lady.'

'I know that.'

'I am sure that you do. Do you believe in the powers of the earth, Jeremy?'

'You mean clairvoyance? Sometimes.'

'Then believe in me. I have the gift. These murders will continue, and the path leads to your door. And to Mrs Hurst's. And to mine. There is no escaping it now.'

I sobered up rather swiftly and lit a cigarette. Normally I didn't smoke on Mondays. 'What do you mean – my door? I'm a reporter, not a policeman.'

He shrugged. 'This is how it will be.'

'What's the point in telling me this? Especially if I can't do anything about it?'

'I did not say you could do nothing about it. The future is not carved in stone. Yet I am seldom wrong about the Ways of Blood. Sometime soon you will meet the man in the mask. And soon after that he will decide to kill you.'

'Why should he?'

He ignored the question. 'It is not you who concerns me. It is Mrs Hurst. I would like you to do something for me. A small thing. In fact, it is but a few spoken words.'

'What? Tell me.'

'I want you to promise to protect her. Even if it means your life.' He leaned forward and waited.

'And that's it?' He nodded. 'You want me to say it?'

'I want you to say it. All of it.'

I shrugged, feeling suddenly foolish. 'I promise to protect her ... with my life, if necessary. Is that it?'

He appeared to relax. 'Thank you,' he said, rising, the

kittens spilling from his lap. 'I will leave you now.' He opened the curtain by the far window and gazed at the sky. 'The rain has stopped and my star is shining.'

'Your star?'

He waved me over and pointed to a bright light below the Plough. 'That is my star. My father gave it to me, a long, long time ago.'

'I hope he also gave you the mineral rights.'

For the first time, Mr Sutcliffe smiled. His teeth were white and even, and his face no longer had the power to cause me fear.

'I like you, Jeremy. I will tell you what I am going to do. I have no sons. So, if you do well, I will give you my star. And all of its mineral rights.'

'That's very good of you. Does it have a name?'

'No,' he said, the smile fading. 'You can name it when it is yours.' He gathered his coat and made for the door.

'Why not stay for a while?' I said. 'Have another coffee or something.'

He shook his head. 'Some people are waiting for me. I will not disappoint them.'

The flat seemed empty without his presence, and strangely quiet. I thought about what he had said, and about the promise I had made. But the events floated in my mind amid a sea of unreality.

A scream sounded from the street behind the house. I ran to the rear window but could see nothing. I didn't want to leave the house. And there were often shouts and horseplay outside. But I knew this was different. There had been real pain caged within that sound. I put on my coat and ran downstairs, out into the night.

All around me, the buildings gleamed like anthracite following rain. Behind my house, I found two youths lying on the pavement, a third kneeling by them. One had blood streaming from his mouth; the other was unconscious, his right arm unnaturally bent.

'What happened?' I asked the third youth as I knelt down beside the unconscious lad.

'It was a bastard nigger,' he said. 'We was only messing about.'

On the pavement beside the unconscious youth lay a hammer. 'You'd better phone for an ambulance,' I said. As I pushed my hand down to lever myself up, my fingers touched a metal wrench. The kneeling youth scooped it up and pushed it into the pocket of his coat.

'You didn't see nothin', right?'

'What is there to see?' I asked. 'What was he like?'

'Big as a bastard house.'

The boy with the broken arm began to moan.

'Ring for an ambulance,' I told the other again. I watched him run to the phone box on the other side of the road. He came back within seconds.

'It's been vandalised,' he said.

'There are a lot of criminals about,' I told him.

He ran off to find another phone, and I sat by the two on the pavement. What on earth had I gotten myself into?

10

Now, in cold black and white, it might sound a little odd that I didn't take Mr Sutcliffe's warnings as seriously as I might have. But you have to remember that I am a journalist. I've met clairvoyants before. Often they're staggeringly correct, but at other times . . .

Take the American prophet Jeane Dixon. She successfully predicted Kennedy's assassination – but she also said that the Third World War would begin in the early 1980s. That notwithstanding, for the first week after Mr Sutcliffe's visit, I made sure all my windows were locked and I slept with a kitchen knife beside my bed.

But then I began to feel ridiculous, and I was giving myself nightmares. I have to admit at this point that I'm not what you would call a man of action. I hate violence of any kind and was never much of a scrapper. I put the knife away the moment I realised I would never be able to plunge it into a human being. And the nightmares stopped.

During the two months that followed, the murders faded from the public consciousness. Front-page leads became down-page items, then switched to the inside news columns to be lost amid the black and white crazy paving of flower shows, burglaries, weddings and obituaries that are the bedrock of a local paper's success.

The front page was now being dominated by increasing unrest in the south of the town. It was a familiar story. The old close-knit community terraced homes had been largely sacked by a rampaging army of town planners. Tower blocks and concrete wastelands sprawled across what was known locally as 'The Estate', although its official name was Lansdowne. Muggings had increased by double percentage figures for the past five years. Rapes, assaults and burglaries in that area rarely made the front page. A page-seven news brief might read: *There were fifteen burglaries on Lansdowne Estate last week, with goods stolen exceeding £8,000.*

No one I had come across lived on the Estate by choice. Unemployment there was high and rising, as was drug abuse. Policing the area was a nightmare, as many officers would admit – but only off the record. Foot patrols were discouraged after several attacks and the police had to accept all kinds of abuse when they ventured into Lansdowne.

'It's like Belfast,' Detective Sergeant Adams told me once. 'You feel like you're part of some occupying army. There's no way to win there. Catch a rapist in the act and some sodding "Coon Is Innocent" committee gets formed and there's hell to pay.' John Adams was not the man to head a race relations committee.

Anyway, the long and the short of it was that a young man arrested following a mugging died in custody from a fractured skull. Several police cars had been stoned and gangs started to congregate in the streets around Lansdowne. Crime soared and an increasing feeling of tragedy ahead coloured our stories.

Ethel's home was on the edge of Lansdowne and mine was only – if you'll pardon the expression – a stone's throw away.

But life went on, much as I guess it did during the Blitz. I still covered weddings and regular news stories. I remained persona non grata among the other reporters. On the home front, my kittens were fast becoming cats and Mrs Simcox had stopped inviting me in for tea, although I almost knocked on her door one day when I heard her crying ...

I continued to work on the murder story, but only intermittently. I met Mrs Bowyer's ex-husband, Jack, when he came into the office to complain about the lack of police activity. I was the only reporter in at the time and I took him to the interview room on the second floor. He was a tall man with greying hair and an athletic stride.

'I want to know what they're doing. It's been weeks now and I can't get any answers.'

'I don't think the killer left any clues,' I said. 'And there are no witnesses.'

'But she was *murdered*,' he said, as if that fact alone should be enough for the police to arrest at least a dozen suspects.

'I'm sorry, Mr Bowyer, but there isn't much the paper can do. I know the officers concerned with the case, and I also know they're doing their best.'

He snorted and shook his head. 'This used to be a decent country,' he said. 'Law-abiding. When I was a boy, there were always bobbies on the street. Murderers didn't get away with it back then.'

I've always been unconvinced by stories of the 'good old days' but decided not to mention Jack the Ripper.

'I'd like to get my bloody hands on him,' he said. His face was flushed a deep red and his eyes shone with distant light. I had a sudden rush of empathy and I knew what he was thinking: if he'd still been living with her, she would be alive.

'Why did you get divorced?' I asked, before I could stop the question rolling from mind to tongue.

He looked up and blinked. 'I fell in love,' he said, 'not that it's any business of yours. I married Dory when I was a lot younger. We got on well but it was no great love match. Then I met Wendy at work, and I guess that was it. But Dory and I stayed friends. Oh, not right away, but after about a year we started seeing each other again. She was a sweet woman. Didn't deserve that.'

'Nobody deserves that,' I said.

He stood then and rubbed his hand over his Clint Eastwood chin.

'I'd just like to know why,' he said.

'Just a nutter.'

'You think so?'

'Who else could do something like that?' I asked him.

He shrugged and left.

I had other stories to complete and put him from my mind. I'd finished two when Bateman returned from lunch. He dropped a ham sandwich on my desk.

'What's that for?'

'Keep your strength up, son. You've been doing well lately. Carry on like this and I might change my opinion of you.'

My teeth snapped together, catching the sarcastic retort on the tip of my tongue as it raced, claws bared, from my mind. 'Thanks,' I said.

He grinned and walked away, stopping in the doorway. 'You seen much of Ethel lately?'

'No, I've been busy. You think I should pop round?'

'Why not – she may have had a dream or something. Worth a try?'

'She's not a fortune teller, Don. And I've got this Stan King business today.'

'Poor bastard,' he said, meaning King. 'Okay. Go and see her tomorrow.'

I returned to my notes. Stan King was a former postman who had fallen ill with cancer. His union had failed to help him with his financial problems, his ex-employers felt they no longer had any reason to support him, and now he was living out his sentence of death. A local councillor had brought us the story as part of the fundraising drive she was spearheading to buy a laser scanner for the local hospital. Such a scanner would have spotted Stan's cancer at a much earlier stage and his life would probably have been saved. Now the cancer had pierced the outer skin of Stan's heart and was inoperable. Equally unfortunate for the poor man was that it had also lodged in his windpipe and was slowly choking him to death. He was only thirty-five, with a young wife and son.

I interviewed him one weekend as we sat in the garden of his home. He wasn't easy to talk to. His words came slowly between corrugated breaths and his eyes were dull and pleading. I felt alien in his company. So did most of his 'friends', apparently, because people rarely called any more, a fact that filled his wife Francine with righteous rage. She was a large woman with rust-coloured hair and green eyes.

'No one wants to look death in the eye,' I said, feeling ashamed, because had it not been for my job, I wouldn't have wished to be there either. She put down the tea towel and half-dried mug and stared out of the kitchen window to where Stan sat dozing in the sunshine.

'He's a good man,' she said. 'Not great, just ordinary. But good. Kind. And it hurts him that his friends are treating him as if he's already dead.'

'Is there anything else I can do?'

'Anything else? What have you done so far? You're going to write about him. So what? That won't help us. If we were rich Americans, we'd be all right. I bet Joan Collins wouldn't be left to suffer like he is.'

I couldn't argue. When I returned to the office, I rang his doctor and put the same point to him.

'There's some truth in it,' he admitted. 'They have laser surgery techniques in Buffalo that beat anything we have.'

'Buffalo?'

'New York.' He gave me the name of the hospital and I added it to my notes.

I ate the ham sandwich Bateman had given me and stared at the name of the American hospital. The other reporters started drifting back from lunch and I closed my notes and began to type the last of my stories. It was nothing special, something about cowboy insulators ripping off pensioners.

By 6.15 p.m. I was alone in the office. I dialled international directory enquiries and obtained the telephone number of the hospital in Buffalo, then rang them. Having stated my business, I was put through to three different people, all of whom left me on hold, before I finally spoke to a Dr Jacqueline Chan. I outlined Stan's condition.

'And why are you contacting me?' she asked, not unpleasantly.

'I was told your hospital has a form of laser surgery unequalled anywhere.'

'That's not strictly true. There's another unit in Houston.'

'If we flew him out to you, what would you charge to treat him?'

'We can't save his life, Mr Miller, and I wouldn't want to raise his hopes.'

'What would you charge?'

'Might I enquire why you're doing this?'

On impulse, I told her about Stan's wife and her comment about Joan Collins. I also mentioned the reaction he was experiencing from friends.

'If you get his specialist to send me the notes, and his

illness is as you've described, we'll treat him for nothing,' she said. 'We're running a research programme and I think he'd fit in. You get him here and we'll enrol him. How does that sound?'

'If you were here, I'd kiss your feet.'

'Remember, don't raise his hopes. At most, he gets a couple of months of life. If we're lucky.'

I thanked her and rang off. Even though it was out of hours I managed to raise Stan's specialist, who promised to send his notes to Dr Chan first thing in the morning.

'One small point, Mr Miller. Stan won't be able to afford the flight.'

He was right about that. The Kings were behind on their mortgage payments and in debt to the tune of around £2,000. I made myself a coffee and rang Don Bateman at home.

'Couldn't this wait until the morning?' he said.

I felt foolish. Of course it could.

'Yes. I'm sorry.'

'Wait!' he called, just as the phone was going down. 'No, I'm sorry, Jeremy. I fell asleep in my chair and I'm always snappy when I wake up. Talk to me.'

I outlined the story – and the problem.

He chuckled. 'You get a top American hospital to take him for nothing and you're worried about air fare? Leave it to me.'

'What will you do?'

'Airlines, my boy, love publicity. We'll get him flown out first class. We'll also front-page the story, which should tug a few heartstrings and open a few wallets. With luck, we may even get his wife out there with him. Shame the bugger's got to die, though. The public love happy endings.'

'He's not dying on purpose,' I snapped.

'What? Well, of course he's not. Don't misunderstand me – I'm as soft as the next man, but this is a story. What I'm really saying is, I wish it could have a happier ending.'

Another phone began ringing. I said goodbye to Bateman and answered it.

'Is that the *Herald*?'

'Yes.'

'Sergeant Taylor here. One of your cars has been in a pile-up on Western Avenue. The driver's in intensive care, but after she was rescued the car caught fire and we've no record of who she is.'

'She?'

'Young woman.' He read out the registration number. It was the editorial pool car. It had to be Sue.

I took down the hospital details and tried to ring Bateman again, but his line was busy. I called the minicab firm the *Herald* had an account with and waited impatiently downstairs for the car to arrive.

11

The hospital reception area was crowded, so I made my way to the wide-bodied lifts and waited for several minutes, watching the flashing yellow arrows. These were clearly designed to mock the gathering throng. One arrow would flicker, pointing downward, indicating the lift was on its way. Like lemmings the crowd would surge towards the glossy steel doors, their eyes locked on the illuminated numbers. Seventh floor, sixth, fifth, fourth, third, fourth. Fourth! An angry murmur would sound and the mocking arrow would now flash upwards. This happened more than once, to growing agitation from the crowd. I controlled my impatience and, finally, as if realising they had no power over me, the steel doors surrendered and whispered open.

I stepped out on the sixth floor, seeking the ward with the deeply uplifting name of South. A student nurse was at the reception desk. She was short, and very young. A badge on her breast proclaimed her to be Student Nurse Donaghue.

'I'm here to see Susan Cater.'

She scanned a list pinned up by a grey phone. 'We have no one here of that name.'

'The car-accident victim. She came in earlier this evening.'

Her eyes showed her concern and filled me with fear. I swallowed hard.

'She's in theatre at the moment. Are you a relative?'

'Brother.'

'Have her parents been informed?'

'She's an orphan.'

'Are you the only relative?'

'Yes.'

'I'll get Doctor Chambers to have a word with you. Would you like to wait out by the lift? You can smoke there.'

'How is she?'

'I don't know,' she said softly, reaching out and squeezing my arm. 'I'll get someone to bring you a cup of tea.'

I looked around, through the entrances of three nearby wards where visitors were sitting, speaking to friends or relatives in hushed whispers. What I had told Nurse Donaghue was true. Sue Cater was an orphan – twice over. Her mother had been a single parent, what with her father dying of TB six weeks before the marriage. Her mother committed suicide when her daughter was three. Sue was taken into care and then adopted by a Sussex family. They had died in a car crash two years ago. There were no brothers or sisters.

I waited almost an hour for the doctor to appear. He was young and fresh-eyed and I hated his apologetic smile.

'I'm sorry I've been so long,' he said. 'Your sister is out of surgery now.'

'How is she?'

'Not good, I'm afraid. She has a fractured skull and some damage to the kidneys. A broken rib pierced her lung. There are other injuries, but the skull worries us most.'

'So what's the prognosis?'

Again the apologetic smile. 'It's not easy to say, Mr Cater. A lot of people would be dead already.'

'But some would recover, yes?'

He spread his hands. 'A small percentage. A very small percentage. The chaplain is with her at the moment. What religion is she?'

'She won't need the last rites,' I said.

He nodded in understanding. 'Would you like to see her?'

'Yes.'

'Her face is a bit of a mess, but it's mostly superficial.'

He led me to a small room marked Ward G. Inside, Sue was lying beside a battery of machines. There was a tube in her nose and a cap had been pulled over her hair. Another tube extended from her left arm. Her face was a mass of purple and yellow bruises and there was a stitched-up gash on her forehead. Her lips were swollen and split, her eyelids black and puffy.

The chaplain smiled as I entered. He was a tubby man with a kindly face. I guess that a kindly face is a prerequisite for his calling.

'There is a chapel on the next floor if you would like to pray,' he said. I barely heard him and didn't see him leave. I pulled up a chair on Sue's right and sat staring at her battered face. Knowing she was unconscious, I reached out and took her hand. I once interviewed a psychic healer who told me that all of us have a power for healing, and that it was possible to pass strength from one person to another through the touching of hands. I thought of him then and willed my health to flow into her. It would be pleasant to recall that I sensed some movement of power, but I didn't. I merely felt the warmth of her fingers, the softness of her skin.

Every so often, nurses entered the room, checked the machines and left again. One brought me a cup of coffee at around 2 a.m. In all that time, Sue didn't move. I slid my fingers to her wrist, feeling for the pulse. It fluttered like a dying butterfly under my touch.

Somewhere during that time, I started to talk to her. The door was closed and I didn't feel self-conscious. I told her first that I was sorry, and then I said that my strength was hers. The words flowed so easily.

At 7 a.m., I left her and rang Don Bateman. He was on his way instantly. Together we saw Dr Chambers, who said the next two days would be critical. Bateman sent me home and told me to take the morning off, but I couldn't. I bathed and shaved, fed the cats and returned to the office. No one felt like working, but we did anyway.

That afternoon, I drove to the edge of Lansdowne and parked outside Ethel's house. She wasn't in, but I saw Mr Sutcliffe working on his roses further along the terrace.

'How are you?' I asked, stopping to admire the blooms.

'I am well, Jeremy. You look tired.'

'Yes. I feel it. Can I use your phone?'

'I do not possess one. Come inside. I will give you some tea.' I followed him into the house, which in structure was identical to Ethel's. But there the resemblance ended. It was like stepping into another world. The walls were covered with wood carvings that could only have been African in origin, and several hide rugs decorated the floor in the lounge. Above the mantel shelf was a strange spear with a two-foot blade and an eighteen-inch haft.

'It is an assegai,' said Mr Sutcliffe.

'It can't be very accurate – the blade's too heavy.'

'It is a stabbing spear. It is not for throwing. It was designed by the great King Chaka. It is a superlative weapon.' He brought me a glass of tea with a slice of lemon floating on the surface. It had an unusual flavour and was very refreshing. He removed his flat brown cap and spread himself in a cane armchair.

'The killer appears to have gone to ground,' I said.

'Not for long.'

I nodded, but didn't believe him.

'What is troubling you, Jeremy?'

'Your star. You said your father gave it to you, but the stars in the Southern Hemisphere are different from those in the North.'

He grinned. 'My father gave me my star in Switzerland, where I went to school. Strangely, it is one of the reasons I now dwell in Europe. I want my star to shine over me when I die.'

'You look very fit to me.'

'Thank you. But I will not die in my bed. Your killer will slay me.'

'Why must you talk like that?' I snapped. 'I was just beginning to relax.'

He chuckled. 'Your race will never understand mine. But no matter. It was in my mind to track him down. But now I cannot, for there is such hatred simmering around me. Can you feel it?'

'You mean the Estate?'

'Yes. There will be bloodshed here. I have told Ethel to take a short holiday. She is in Devon.'

'I thought things were settling down.'

'There are those among us who do not want "things to settle down". They will have their day. Do not come around here for a while, Jeremy. It will be unpleasant.'

I finished my tea and said nothing. There was an eerie calm inside Mr Sutcliffe's home that was more than mildly disturbing, as if the difference between us that he spoke of was somehow manifested by the carvings and the rugs and the broad-bladed stabbing spear.

My mind switched to thoughts of Sue Cater, lying alone in a hospital bed, hovering between life and death. I needed to find a telephone.

'Is she a friend?' he asked.

'Yes,' I answered, a fraction of a second before the shock hit me. 'Do you read minds?'

'No. Would you like me to help her?'

'In what way?'

'In the only way that matters.'

'You're a healer?'

'We are all healers. It is part of the earth magic.'

I didn't know what to say. Part of me anticipated the acute embarrassment of allowing Mr Sutcliffe into the room under the sceptical stares of the medical staff, but another part was ready to grasp at any straw.

'Yes. Would you like to come with me?'

'I will see you there this evening.'

'They're only allowing relatives into the room.'

'Of course. I will be there at nine.' I had the absurd vision of Mr Sutcliffe arriving in ceremonial costume. I thrust it away.

Outside his house, four black youths were lounging against the car. It was a spare advertising vehicle with the *Herald* banner on each door.

I moved around towards the driver's door. A tall youth blocked my way. His eyes were large, piercing and angry.

'What the fuck you wan'?' he said.

'I don't want anything from you. Would you move out of the way?'

'You wan' fuckin' make me?' he snarled, pushing me in the chest.

Mr Sutcliffe appeared behind the youth, his huge hand descending on his collar. The fingers appeared to flick outwards and the thug hurtled into the road, landing on his shoulder. The other three moved forwards menacingly. Mr Sutcliffe ignored them.

'Nice to see you again, Jeremy. Remember what I said.'

I hesitated, my eyes on the thugs.

'Just drive away. There will be no trouble from these children.'

I took him at his word, climbed in and started the engine. I believed him. Next to Mr Sutcliffe, the youths looked almost insubstantial.

Back at the office, I saw Don Bateman, who had just returned from the hospital. 'It doesn't look good, goddammit!' he said.

I made him a coffee and we sat in the editor's office. 'Some joyrider swerved in front of her and her car overturned. A bank clerk dragged her from the wreck just before the whole thing went up.'

I would have given my right arm to be that bank clerk.

'Phil's interviewed the man and we've got a lovely picture.'

'Let's hope there's a happy ending,' I said.

'She's a good girl. Strong. Strong,' he said again, more softly. 'And she's not had much bastard luck in her life. Good of you to sit with her last night.'

'It wasn't any trouble.'

'Okay. You going tonight?'

'Yes. With a friend.' I felt my face redden, but I couldn't bring myself to tell Bateman about Sutcliffe.

'I'll see you there. By the way, the air tickets are all set up for Stan King and his wife. You want to be the one who tells them?'

'No. Andrew's good at that sort of thing.'

'You're not good with compliments, are you, Jeremy? Or gratitude.'

'No. But I'm really good at being a total prat.'

'Knowing it is half the battle, son. You'll be all right.'

12

Jeremiah Gibson stood with his colleagues outside the terraced house, his mind full of righteous indignation. As head of the Neighbourhood Action Alliance, he'd grown used to being a man of some influence, and enjoyed the fact that radio and television crews contacted him for comments and interviews when trouble erupted on the Lansdowne. The cause of the trouble was easy to understand. The police were racist to a man and constantly affronted the dignity of the local population with their harassment and their stop-and-search routines. As far as Jeremiah Gibson was concerned, they were the enemy.

The main enemy, anyway. Because there were other enemies within the community. The fainthearts, and those crawling, fawning objects who couldn't shake their genetic memories of kowtowing to a white society.

Jeremiah, at 56, was a tall, wide-shouldered man, bald and bearded, who adored his grandchildren calling him Mr T after the star of *The A-Team*. He glanced around at the four men with him and smiled reassuringly at his son.

Earlier that day, he had watched the local newspaper car pull into the kerb and had expected the occupant to knock at his own door. Instead, he'd gone to the home of the surly giant whose disgusting affair with the old white woman was the talk of the neighbourhood. Jeremiah had sent his son to ask the journalist his business; a reasonable request from one of the leading figures in the community. But his son had been abused by the reporter and then attacked by the giant. This was not to be tolerated.

He opened the gate to Mr Sutcliffe's home and walked up the short pathway to the front door. It opened and a tall figure loomed ahead of Jeremiah. He looked into amber eyes flecked with gold, and drew himself up to his full height. It galled him that he still had to look up at the man.

'You struck my son,' he said. 'I saw you from my window.'

The giant smiled, but it was not reassuring. 'Your son is a thug. Had I struck him, he would not now be standing here. I merely brushed him away as I would a troublesome insect.'

Suddenly, Jeremiah was at a loss. He was used to respect, but this man offered none. A man behind Jeremiah pushed forward.

'I'll deal with the motherfucker!' he shouted and hurled himself at Mr Sutcliffe, coming to a dead stop as a huge hand met his throat, the fingers closing like a steel trap around his windpipe. He saw a fist raised before his eyes, then the lights went out. Mr Sutcliffe dropped the body, which slumped to the ground.

'Take him away from here,' said Mr Sutcliffe. 'And do not come back.' His voice was edged with boredom and his eyes burned into Jeremiah's.

'You think you can get away with this kind of behaviour?' stormed Jeremiah.

'I think I just did. Now go away and plan your ludicrous war. And in case my tone does not make it clear to you, let me explain it simply: I despise you. I despise your stupidity. I despise your cowardice. You are not fit to walk among men. Go!'

Jeremiah watched as the giant moved back into his

shadowed hallway. The door clicked shut. A man behind him lifted a half-brick.

'No!' said Jeremiah. 'He will come to see the error of his ways. I'll make sure of that.'

Two men hauled the unconscious attacker to his feet.

Inside the house, Mr Sutcliffe sat cross-legged on the floor, his eyes closed, his heart racing. Deep, steady breathing reduced the anger in his soul, massaging the hatred from his heart. He had come thousands of miles to lose this hatred – this emotion he had tried to drown in blood in the jungles of Mozambique and Zimbabwe, in the killer-camps of Angola. But blood could not wash away hatred. Nor could the rolling thunder of the Kalashnikov AK-47 overpower it, as the rounds tore into living flesh at 2,300 feet per second.

For a few minutes, Mr Sutcliffe ceased to be and Mangiwe Mazui squatted in the bush once more, his flat cap shading his eyes, his AK-47 trained on the road. The lorry trundled into view and a young blond driver was about to light a cigarette when the shell tore off the top of his head. Men leapt from the rear of the truck as the first clatter of gunfire erupted. Mangiwe raked the group, put in a fresh clip and melted back into the bush, leaving the screams of the wounded and dying behind him.

When Robert Mugabe raised his arms in triumph at the end of the war, Mangiwe had been filled with a terrible rage. The country should have been ruled by the Matabele, not the dung-eating Mashona. But it was not to be. Mangiwe smashed his AK-47 against a rock and burned his combat fatigues. Rhodesia was dead. The Matabele would never rule the green land again.

Mangiwe left the bush and journeyed in search of his father's star.

Mr Sutcliffe opened his eyes and focused on the assegai above the mantel shelf, and the vase of roses beneath it.

Death would come soon. But not soon enough.

Never soon enough.

Back home, I'd just fed the cats and settled down to sleep when the doorbell rang. I glanced at my watch. It was almost 3 a.m. At the front door was Detective Sergeant John Adams.

'Sorry to bother you at this time of the night, Jeremy, but we can't locate Mrs Hurst.'

'Why do you need her?'

'There's been another killing. And a police officer has been murdered.'

He looked more tired than I felt. I invited him in and made him a coffee.

'If I had the money,' he said suddenly, 'I'd move to the south coast and open a newsagent's.' He rubbed at his eyes, leaned back on the sofa and flicked open the curtain. 'It won't be long, you know, before the lid really blows off Lansdowne.'

'Ray Morris was on the radio tonight denying racism in the local force,' I told him.

'I know. Bloody funny world, isn't it? Last year we were reprimanded for issuing statistics that showed eighty-seven per cent of muggings in the Estate were done by blacks. Racist, that was, apparently. But the truth doesn't count any more.'

'If I remember the report correctly, over eighty per cent of the victims were also black. Hardly surprising in Lansdowne. And if you want some more statistics, seventy per cent of black muggers get prison sentences against only twenty-six per cent of white offenders.'

'Fucking statistics,' he hissed. 'What do they tell you? If you've got your head in an oven and your feet in a fridge, you'll be comfortable all over. You can't get away from the facts, though. Lansdowne is a nightmare – and it'll only get worse. Softly, softly! If I hear that phrase one more time—'

'You were asking about Ethel?'

He drained his coffee. 'Yes. Two of our officers spotted a man on the edge of the Estate at 1.45 a.m. this morning. He ran when they told him to stop, so they chased him. He stabbed one of them to death and then got away. We think it was the killer. No, goddammit, we *know* it was the killer. Mrs Hurst had him pegged down to the last detail – black sweater, combat fatigues, balaclava mask. He'd just killed his third victim.'

'Who was she?'

'Black woman. Agnes Veronia. And get this, Jeremy – she was trying to commit suicide. He brought her round before topping her.'

'That's insane!'

'You think killing women with an upholstery needle and stitching them up isn't?'

'That's not what I meant,' I told him. 'It's late, and I'm tired. Look, Ethel is in Devon for a few days. As soon as she gets back, I'll let you know.'

'Whereabouts in Devon?'

'I've no idea, John. You might try her neighbour, Mr Sutcliffe. Two doors down on the left.'

'Big black man?'

'Yes. You know him?'

'You could say that we are aware of his existence. Okay. Thanks for the coffee.' He stood and almost stumbled.

'You should get some rest,' I said, rising with him.

'Yeah, that would be nice. But DI Fletcher comes back and he'll want to hear we've made some progress on the murder. See you soon, Jeremy.'

'Look after yourself,' I told him.

14

The meeting had been going on for only half an hour, but already the conference room was thick with smoke. Ray Morris was tired, and with that fatigue came a tight, barely controlled anger. His exhaustion wasn't surprising given that he'd been awoken in the early hours of the morning with the news that Constable Richard Bealey had been stabbed to death on Lansdowne Estate and another woman murdered. Eleven hours after he'd left his warm bed and his cold wife, the clues were still being assembled.

Agnes Veronia, a thirty-five-year-old West Indian woman, had been killed by a long needle plunged into the base of her skull and her genital area had been stitched together with black thread. A suicide note had been found next to the body, and, according to the pathologist, the victim had swallowed enough Mogadon to kill her twice over. As with the previous two murders, the killer had called the station, and this time his voice had been recorded.

Morris silenced the group and asked for a window to be opened. Detective Sergeant Adams obliged. Frank Beard eased his huge bulk back on the flimsy chair and poured a glass of water. Alexander Stevens, the department's go-to psychiatrist, lit another cigarette from the still-burning stub of the last.

'Piece it together again, John,' Morris told Adams.

'Well, sir, the killer arrived at Mrs Veronia's flat at between midnight and 1 a.m. He broke the safety chain and found her in bed. The sheet was half on the bed and half on the floor pointing to the door, so we surmise he dragged her to the bathroom. Her hair was wet, and it looks like he tried to revive her before killing her. He left the flat somewhere before 1.35 a.m. and was seen running along Manor Road by Officers Bealey and Congrave. Bealey gave chase on foot, while Congrave took the car and tried to cut him off at the old iron bridge. The killer doubled back and killed Bealey. Congrave found the body and radioed in.'

'Who's with Bealey's wife?'

'WPC Langhorne, sir.'

'What do you make of it, Alex?'

The psychiatrist removed his glasses. 'There's still some way to go before I can give you a definitive answer to that question, but I'd say the killer is punishing the women for some perceived crime. He tried to wake her before executing her, so there was obviously a need for her to know she was being punished. Death itself wasn't enough. We now have three female victims – all divorcees, all close to middle age.'

'Could they all have belonged to some lonely-hearts club?' asked Beard.

'No evidence of that so far,' replied Adams.

'If I may continue?' snapped Stevens. 'The method of execution is relatively painless, and he always cleans the victims afterwards. The sewing up of the genital area is interesting, as is the instrument he uses. I think it's more of a statement, and a relatively simple one – he's "stitching them up" after "giving them the needle". One can only assume that he feels these women have "stitched him up" in some way. He's obviously a man of some intelligence, twisted though it might be.'

'He's also left-handed,' said Adams, 'judging by the

94

blow that killed Bealey. And very strong. Congrave said he thought the man was around six-one and moved like an athlete. He only saw the face for a fraction of a second, but that was long enough to register the man was white. He was also wearing black combat trousers and a dark sweater.'

'What about the tape recording?' asked Morris, swinging to the last man in the group, a short, balding figure in an old Harris Tweed jacket.

'We've identified most of the background sounds,' he said, 'but there's nothing useful. And all he said was, "Another dead one at Three-Three-Two Exeter Towers." London accent, clipped but well enunciated, of a well-educated man around twenty-five to thirty-five years of age. Interesting the way he said "three-three-two" and not "three hundred and thirty-two". He's probably someone who does a lot of business by phone. Apart from that, there's little to say.'

'But he wasn't wearing his balaclava when he killed Bealey?' asked Morris.

'Not as far as we know,' said Adams. 'Do you want me to contact the psychic lady?'

Morris nodded. 'But keep it quiet.'

'Yes, sir.'

'One last thing, Superintendent,' said Alex Stevens. 'The use of the words "another dead one" – there's no suggestion of finality. You can expect him to strike again.'

'I think we all know that, Alex,' Morris said darkly.

15

Ethel sat on the crowded Tube, her beige leather suitcase beside her. Standing immediately before her were three youths with pink and white hair raised into giant plumes like the crests on Roman soldiers' helmets. On her left, a man was reading the *Evening Standard*, and every time he turned a page, his hand came close to touching her knee. Ethel didn't like the Tube. The train journey from Devon had been pleasant and she'd sat in the buffet car watching the green countryside floating by, the sunlight streaming in slanted pillars from behind cotton-wool clouds. It was such a civilised way to travel, she thought. But the Tube!

Somewhere to her right sat a man who had obviously been recently smoking a pipe and the strong, acrid scent drifted through the airless cylinder that made up the body of the carriage and mingled with the other odours: stale sweat, hot feet, cheap perfumes and unwashed clothes.

Her excitement at being summoned back to London was fading fast. The train drew into Hammersmith and Ethel watched as the posters on the walls outside eased from a rainbow blur to subliminal flashes, and finally to recognisable images.

The crush around her eased and the remainder of the journey was made in relative comfort. She found herself longing to be home with a fresh pot of tea, and for the chance to sit and chat with Mr Sutcliffe, listening to his softly told tales of life in Rhodesia between the wars.

Normally, Ethel travelled home by bus from the station, but today she felt extravagant and settled herself in a taxi. The driver was a fat, surly-faced individual who drove too fast until he came to the road adjoining hers. Then he slowed down, manoeuvring the Granada around the bricks and debris littering the street. Mr Sutcliffe's house displayed a broken window, covered now with plywood.

'This is as far as I go, lady,' said the driver. 'There's a mass of broken glass ahead.' Ethel paid him and walked slowly to her home, picking her way through the bricks, stones and smashed bottles. She looked up at the windows of the houses opposite hers and saw several faces peering coldly at her.

Once inside, she unpacked her suitcase and put on the kettle. For the first time in years, she was not glad to be home.

As the kettle was boiling, Mr Sutcliffe tapped on the front door. Ethel let him in. A year ago, she'd given him a key so that he could perform his odd jobs without having to wait for her if she were out. But he never used it while she was home.

'It looks dreadful outside,' she said.

He removed his flat brown cap. 'It is only the beginning, Mrs Hurst.'

She shook her head and ushered him into the lounge before fetching the tea tray. Mr Sutcliffe's large pottery mug had long since looked perfectly at ease with her bone china cup and saucer, echoing their own relationship. She passed the mug to him. 'What happened to your window?'

'Some men broke in. It was nothing.'

'You didn't hurt them, did you?'

'I had little choice, Mrs Hurst. They were armed with clubs and knives.'

'Why did they attack you?'

He smiled. 'I do not know. Perhaps it is God mocking me. I am not a popular man in Lansdowne. How was your holiday?'

'Devon is lovely, especially at this time of year. And I saw Mr Clover – you remember him?'

'Yes. The postman. Is he well?'

'He's very happy. He has a cottage near a bay. I had tea with him. He sends his regards and hopes you will travel down to see his rose garden one of these days.'

'You are home early.'

'I had a message from the police. They wanted me to return to London urgently but wouldn't tell me what it's all about. I can guess, though – I saw in the morning papers that another woman has been killed.'

'And a policeman.'

'Oh dear. It's beginning to look as if you were correct, Mr Sutcliffe. There's nothing I can do.' Ethel poured a second cup of tea and leaned back in the armchair.

Mr Sutcliffe shook his head and smiled. 'That is not what I said. I said he would kill again. And he has. But you can still be instrumental in stopping him. I advised you against it, not because I felt you would be unable to assist the police, but because I did not want to see you in danger. Now, as you would say, your hat is in the ring. Now we must catch him.'

'He was on the front page of the newspapers,' said Ethel. 'They're calling him Deathmask.'

Mr Sutcliffe held back the obscenity hovering behind his lips.

'Soon,' he said, 'they will be wearing T-shirts acclaiming

him. Then the filmmakers will seek to glorify his life. I am getting old. I can no longer accept with equanimity the lunacies of this age.'

'It was never any different,' said Ethel. 'The gladiators fought for the crowds. It's just that the arena is so much larger now. You know, when I was a little girl, all the houses around here had their front doors open all day. We used to run in and out of people's homes. I thought those days had gone for ever. But I went for a walk to the Green last week, and I passed the Exeter Towers part of the Estate. Lots of doors were open and there were children playing, just like I used to.'

'It is not the same. You had no evil eye then,' he said, pointing to the television.

'I hardly think *Crossroads* encourages muggers,' said Ethel.

'You know that is not what I mean. I killed my first man during the war. He was running across a field, bent low. For a second or two, I could not pull the trigger. When I did, he just pitched to the earth, unmoving. For several days I could think of nothing else. Then I killed my second man, then the third. The more death I created, the less it touched me. It was the same in Matabeleland. We are all ruled by our emotions, and that … thing … sits like a devil, twisting us day by day. Endless bodies in little wars. Then the news ends and the dramas begin. More bodies and death. A rape here, a murder there. Then back to the news.'

'We have had this conversation before, Mr Sutcliffe, and it always annoys you.'

He sank back into his chair. 'You are correct as always, Mrs Hurst. I have lived my life and have no cause to lambast this age of envy and stupidity. I helped to create it.'

'You were never evil. I know that. How are your roses?'

'Someone tore off all the blooms, but they will grow again.'

'There's a lesson in that, I think,' she said, reaching for the phone. 'I had better see what the police want from me.'

16

The driver watched as she came out of the supermarket carrying two heavy bags, her blonde hair held in place by a braided headband. She was slender yet heavy-breasted, the model of the Hollywood sex symbol.

'Who are you trying to kid?' he whispered. She was wearing a red tracksuit top, tight-fitting blue jeans and white trainers, and she looked no more than twenty-five. But he knew different. She was thirty-seven years old and maintained her figure with aerobics classes three times a week in the Old Warehouse complex. And she jogged in the park on Wednesdays and Saturdays in a designer tracksuit.

It had taken him some time to run her to ground. She hadn't reverted to her maiden name. She'd married again – the bitch. That marriage had also failed, but she kept her second husband's name even after he died. The single-decker bus pulled up, obscuring his view of her, but he saw the flash of her red tracksuit as she took a seat at the back.

Home to a cup of coffee and perhaps a meeting with her spade lover, thought the driver. *Slag, bitch, cow, slut, whore!*

No! No anger now. Calm. So very calm.

Because I know something you don't know, bitch.

I know when you are going to die.

17

I'd never liked DI Fletcher. There was something about the man that was cold, even emotionless, but I couldn't say what it was. He had regular looks, a square chin and prematurely grey hair. His eyes were blue and frank, his mouth a thin line, and he seemed to say everything through closed teeth. Perhaps it was that he never smiled. Perhaps it was his years as a policeman, with his cynicism growing daily. Whatever the reason, he left you feeling as if you'd just been caught in the act. He was in his early forties and, that rarest of loathsome objects, a chain-smoker fit enough to run half-marathons, which he did in reasonable times.

That Thursday he was sitting at the back of Ray Morris's office, watching as Ethel readied herself for the gruesome task ahead. I'd been hoping he'd look sceptical, and then I could watch gleefully as Ethel wiped the smirk from his face. No such luck. He was charm itself. And somehow that was worse, for I could feel him laughing inside.

Ray Morris and Frank Beard were seated side by side. Don Bateman, Ethel and I faced them across the wide desk on which lay two wedding rings, one a thick band, the other a slender braid of golden wires.

'I'd like to thank you, Mrs Hurst,' said Morris. 'I know this won't be easy for you.'

Ethel smiled, but I could see the lines of tension around her eyes, and I realised for the first time that she was frightened. And then it hit me – why shouldn't she be? She was about to relive a murder, feel it happen to her. She lifted her right hand and gently rubbed at her temple. Then she took a deep breath and reached for the thick wedding ring. Her slender fingers hovered over it, and the hand withdrew. She asked for a glass of water. I fetched it, and tried to smile reassuringly. She picked up the ring, leaned back, her eyes closed. 'I am in a car,' she said. 'I'm smoking a cigarette, and I'm thinking about a game of football. I missed a penalty. We lost. The car is moving slowly. There is a man jogging. Something's not right. I glance at my watch. Almost two in the morning. I wind down the window and call to him. He turns, then sprints away. "Get to the bridge," I tell Ralph, and I jump from the car and start to run. He's a quick bugger, but he's got a surprise in store. He makes the bridge and I go up after him. I can hear the car screeching to a stop. I get to the top, and he's not there. I can see the end of the bridge highlighted by the street lamps. I run forwards. Oh, God! He was crouching. It's him! He's holding the mask! Death! I'm hit. It's him! Something hot. Dark … dark.'

Ethel slumped forwards, the ring tumbling from her hand to roll across the green-carpeted floor. Bateman grabbed her just as she was about to fall from the chair.

Ray Morris ran around the desk. 'Is she all right?'

Ethel's eyes opened. 'I think so,' she said.

'Jesus!' said Bateman. Her right eye was full of blood.

'How do you feel, Mrs Hurst?' asked Morris.

'It was terrible. That poor man.'

'Did you see the killer? His face?' asked Morris.

'No. He was hiding in the dark, and I only caught a glimpse from the car. He was very tall, over six feet. And I think he had light-coloured hair, but I couldn't be sure. The moonlight was very bright.'

'Was there anything else, Mrs Hurst?'

'He's left-handed. And yes, there is something, but I can't make much sense of it. As he stabbed me … him, I mean… his hand touched me. In that moment, there was a mass of images, all blurred. And there was regret. But there was a blue car, and an accident at night involving a child's bicycle. It was all so fast.'

'You think the killer has a blue car?'

'Yes. Large.'

'Anything else?' asked DI Fletcher.

'No … wait – perhaps. Two rose bushes planted close together in a garden. They are important to him, I don't know why, but they were also in his mind. And I see a hanged man. It is an old image, faded, the detail almost forgotten. But it haunts him. That's it, I am afraid. There's something wrong, though, a difference from the last time I was with you. I wish I could explain it.'

'Please try,' said Frank Beard.

'It's like looking in a mirror,' she said. 'What we see is sort of reversed. Only … No. I'm just tired. Let me have the other ring.'

For several minutes, Ethel tried to focus on Agnes Veronia's wedding band, but could see nothing but deep, dark barbiturate dreams.

Ethel's eye injury was caused by a burst blood vessel and it cleared up before too long, but the memory of her eyes opening will never leave me. It was quite the most chilling sight I had ever seen. A taxi took Ethel home, and I was allowed to remain with Bateman and the police officers. My fingers itched to note every detail of the meeting, and to write it up as a feature. But Bateman's word was his bond, and that was no bad thing.

'She's remarkable,' said Morris. 'I've never seen the like. What do you think, Mark?'

DI Fletcher shrugged. 'Too weird for me, sir. Can I see you when the meeting's over?'

Morris nodded. A middle-aged woman brought a tray of plastic cups containing weak coffee without sugar, and we sat listening to the tape Beard had made of Ethel's experience. It was more chilling the second time around, a disembodied voice echoing tinnily from the recorder. When it was finished, Bateman leaned forward.

'So what avenues are left to you, Ray?'

'All known sex offenders are being investigated, but his MO is unlikely to be on file. I've never heard of it before. We've also checked local haberdashery shops for sales of large upholstery needles. Nothing unusual there. House-to-house calls are still ongoing in the area, but we're as welcome in Lansdowne as a shit sandwich.'

'So all you have,' said Bateman, 'is a killer who specialises in divorcees?'

'That's about it.'

'But how does he pick them?' I asked.

'They were all married in April 1975,' said Morris. 'That has to be important, but I'm buggered if I know why. They were each married in separate places, one on April 5th, another on ...' he checked his files '... April 11th, and the last on April 28th. One was a Catholic, the other two were register-office jobs. What's so bloody special about April?'

'A lot of people marry in April,' said Bateman. 'Time was, the paper would stockpile all the wedding announcements for that month and carry them in a four-page spread at the end of April.'

'Well, he's going to make a mistake sooner or later,' said Morris. 'I just hope it's sooner.'

We finished our coffees and Bateman and I walked back along the High Street together. It was a hot, muggy day and I could feel the sweat trickling between my shoulder blades.

It had been days since Sue Cater had come out of the coma, and I'd not been back to see her. I'd visited Mr Sutcliffe to thank him, but he was in a morose mood and I didn't stay long.

At the office, Bateman picked up his messages then stopped dead. 'What a prat I am!' he said. 'And you. And the coppers. We're *all* prats.'

'What is it?'

'I've got a bad back, Jeremy, so you bring that file upstairs.' He pointed to the row of *Herald* back issues, and the answer hit me like a hammer blow. The 1975 file, with its four pages of weddings in one of the April editions!

In Bateman's small office, we cleared his desk of its typewriter, sundry packets of cigarettes, paper clips, notebooks, two ashtrays and several old copies of the *Guardian*. I laid the file down.

'It doesn't feel so long ago to me,' said Bateman, 'but what you're looking at is a historical relic. In those days, the paper was hot metal, and there were no computers, wax bromides or paste-up boards – well, not for us, anyway.' He flipped open the leather-edged cover and we looked down at the front page of the first issue of January 1975. The lead story was about a man without legs who was climbing the Matterhorn. The report was by Don Bateman.

'Good piece,' I said.

'Yes. He made it, too. Gutsy bugger. Must look him up.' He flipped through the issues until he reached the last week of April, and there they were: thirty-four small pictures on a four-page spread under the tinted banner headline APRIL'S WEDDING BELLES.

Agnes Veronia was the first to catch my eye. She was one of only two black women featured. Her maiden name was Cutter, and she'd married at Saint Peter's. I stared hard at the handsome man beside her. They looked like all the other couples pictured, radiantly happy. I felt like a time traveller. Ahead of this woman lay misery, divorce and murder. But on that April day, how different the world must have looked to her. Barbara Davies was next, centre page, arm in arm with Gary Sinclair; twelve years later, he'd be calling her a selfish cow who had come close to ruining his life. The last I spotted was Dorothy Mitchelson. The picture showed her and husband Jack Bowyer cutting a three-tiered cake. Bowyer looked much then as he did now: tall, athletic and confident. If he was to be believed, at the moment this picture was taken he wasn't in love with the woman in white beside him. How different her life might have been had he found the courage to tell her that before the wedding.

'Would we still have the original photographs, Don?'

'No. Just like now, they were contributed by the couples or their families, to be sent back after use. And the blocks are no good to us – as I said, they were all metal in those days and mostly melted down for reuse.'

'Then what good is the file?'

'You still don't see it, do you? The killer is using the same four-page spread. He has to be. Somewhere on these pages is the next victim. Otherwise why are they all from April '75?'

'That's not a bad theory,' I said. 'But how does he know which couples are divorced? We don't carry divorce announcements.'

'I have no idea, Jeremy, but I'm taking a photocopy of this file to Ray Morris. With luck, the next time the bastard strikes the police will be waiting. In the meantime, I want every one of these women checked out.'

'Hell of a feature.'

'It's not a feature. Not yet. We can't openly interview them, just in case I'm wrong. The last thing I want is to draw attention to a load of potential new victims.'

'We're never going to be able to fit this into work time. It's hard enough getting the paper out as it is.'

'A good journalist is a twenty-four-hour man,' he told me.

My first job was as a lorry driver's mate, delivering soft drinks to cafés. There was more money in it, and fewer hours. Still, lorry drivers rarely had the chance to track down murderers.

'You talked me into it. How do I start?'

'First clear your notebook and write up all your stories, then come back and help me. I'll get going now.'

'I won't be around this afternoon – we're taking Stan King to Heathrow.'

He swore. 'Call me at home this evening.'

It didn't take long to clear my notebook of seven news briefs and a short piece about a new scout hut. It was coming up to 1.15 p.m. when Martin Dunn's limousine drew up outside the office. Martin was a local businessman who had made a fortune in the early-eighties computer boom. Every time we carried a sad story, Martin came up with some cash. This time he'd offered £1,000 for Stan King's wife, Francine, to fly with him to Buffalo. He'd also arranged the limousine and a chauffeur, and someone to look after the Kings' kid. The other pleasant point to recall is that Martin always insisted his donations remained anonymous, which endeared him to the editorial staff.

I rode in the limo to Stan's home. He was still deeply in debt, but the building society had frozen his mortgage repayments, winning themselves some valuable publicity in the process. Francine was waiting in the doorway when we arrived.

'You're late,' she said. Gratitude was not Francine's strong suit. But then she saw this as a stunt for the newspaper, which I guess it was, although I knew that the staff cared and had contributed almost £100 to the fund that would see Francine ensconced in a decent motel during Stan's visit. Still, she knew this wasn't a 'miracle' trip. At best, the dying Stan would be able to struggle to breathe for a few months longer.

Stan was sitting on a sofa in the lounge. He looked tired and extraordinarily thin. He smiled when I came in.

'How are you feeling?' I asked.

'Scared ... of flying.' He grinned.

Francine helped him into a wheelchair while the chauffeur transferred their suitcases to the car. She wheeled him down the short drive and I opened the limo's rear door. Stan rose on shaking legs and Francine manoeuvred him onto the soft leather seat, then climbed in beside him. She had to get out again when neither I nor the chauffeur could collapse the wheelchair. She looked at us as if we were a pair of clumsy idiots.

On the M4, I swung around to see how Stan was coping with the journey. His chemotherapy tended to make him travel-sick.

'We could have taken a cab,' said Francine. 'Might have had more money in America, then.'

'The car was donated free,' I said.

'Pity whoever it was didn't add some cash.'

'He added a thousand pounds.'

'I expect he's getting some publicity out of it.'

'With respect, Mrs King, you really are a graceless cow.'

I turned away, my face burning. I glanced at the driver. His left hand lifted from his lap in a thumbs-up sign, then he pressed a button and a glass screen hissed shut, cutting us off from the passengers in the rear.

'I reckon the poor bastard got cancer on purpose,' said the driver, 'rather than face life with that harridan.'

'She does have a way of getting under the skin,' I replied. We hadn't said much on the short drive to Stan's house, so I introduced myself.

'I can't shake hands,' he said, steering the car into the fast lane, 'but I'm Martin Dunn.'

I admit I was taken aback. 'You don't look anything like the photographs in the office,' I said. 'And I didn't expect you to be the chauffeur.'

'Well, I have to admit, I wanted to see the patient. And I had nothing else planned for this afternoon.'

'What made you offer all that money?'

'Because I've got it, Jeremy. More than I can ever spend. And it's a nice feeling, helping people out. Selfish, really, I suppose, but it gives me pleasure. Plus it's a lot better to read about people caring for a man like Stan than it is to read about riots on Lansdowne or rapes or violence. You agree?'

'Who wouldn't?'

'How long have you been with the *Herald*?'

'Eight months. I was born in West London, but I served my indentures in Kent.'

'Shame about Sue Cater. Nice girl. How's she getting on?'

'Not bad. There's some weakness in her left side and her vision gets blurred, but she's lucky to be alive.'

'She was the first one to talk me into charity work. Some pensioner who couldn't pay the rent. She walked into my office and asked for five hundred quid.'

'Just like that?'

'Almost. I'm glad she did.'

Martin swung the car across the lanes expertly and we cruised off the motorway and into Heathrow. At the terminal, we were met by a British Airways official and our photographer, Jerry. Stan and Francine were whisked through the formalities and we got a good picture of Stan with his thumbs raised next to a 747.

I wished him luck, just before he was taken into the First Class lounge.

'Thanks, Jeremy – for everything. And don't mind Francine. Thank everyone back home for me. Make up a quote or something to say how grateful I am. I'm not too good with words.'

We didn't stay to watch the plane take off but went back into the terminal. Martin bought me a beer and we sat together quietly. He was a handsome man, deceptively built. At first glance, he looked quite slim, but his shoulders and arms were powerful, and he moved with that liquid grace you find in sportsmen. It turned out he was once an apprentice professional footballer with Tottenham, and he still played every Sunday in the Sportsmen's League.

'I never would have made the grade as a pro,' he said. 'Couldn't tackle. And I hated getting kicked. I think the expression most used was "no bottle".' He laughed as he said it.

'I could never see the point of galloping around chasing a pig's bladder wrapped in leather,' I told him.

He was good company, and not much older than me – I was twenty-four, he was twenty-seven. The only real difference between us was about two and a half million pounds.

He drove me home and suggested we meet for a drink the following evening.

It was after seven before I remembered to ring Don

Bateman, for the 'unpaid overtime' work. There was no reply and I settled down for a quiet evening at home.

Bateman rang me at 11.02 pm.

'Weren't asleep, were you?' he asked.

'Don't worry about it. I had to get up to answer the phone anyway. So, what's the plan?'

18

Bateman's plan was relatively simple. Of the thirty-four couples married in April 1975, three women were dead. That left thirty-one. He would check eleven of the surviving women, Deedes and I ten each. As luck would have it, I had two Smiths and a Jones in my ten, plus a Miller and a White. I started the following day with the easiest: Mr and Mrs Coccaciou. In the photograph of 1975, Mrs Brenda Coccaciou was small, dumpy and darkly pretty. Twelve years later, she looked like a female shot-putter.

She invited me into her detached house in the east of town and listened patiently as I spun a yarn about an upcoming feature on the rate of divorces in West London over the last ten years.

'We won't, of course, be naming people we speak to,' I assured her. 'We're just gathering statistics.'

'And why have you come to me?' she asked.

'Well, I was scanning the Electoral Register and I noticed there was no mention of Mr George Coccaciou.'

'He died,' she said. 'Three years ago. Heart attack.'

'I see. I'm sorry to have troubled you.'

'It is not any trouble. We had five beautiful children. They are all doing well. George had a big insurance policy. But you want to know why I think so many people get divorced?' She didn't wait for an answer. 'It is sex. Everyone expects so much from it, and they are always disappointed. And men are like children. They always need new toys to play with. Take my George … He thought I didn't know about the little tart in Hammersmith. Pah! Of course I knew. But did I care? No. People say we marry for love, and respect. Rubbish. A man marries so he can have somewhere warm to put his willie every night.'

For at least an hour, she held forth on the subject, and I dutifully noted her every opinion. After that, I crossed her off my list and began the long search for the others.

I discussed the problem during my meeting with Martin Dunn at the Squash Club bar that evening, where he'd invited me for a drink.

'You're doing this the long way round,' he said. 'Have you never heard of computers?'

'Of course, but how could they help?'

'All the local council records are now on disk, thanks to a certain company I happen to run. I still have access. Which means you can use a search/find protocol and the computer will do your hunting for you. Take the name Smith, for example. By itself, the surname's a problem, but "Sarah Smith" gives you five more characters. I take it you're using the Electoral Register?'

'Yes.'

'Give me the names and I'll have answers for you by tomorrow afternoon.'

I couldn't believe my luck, and I asked if I could watch while he did my work for me.

He grinned. 'Why not? I've always wanted to play detective.'

'Do we have to go to the town hall?'

'No. We'll do it from my office. Sounds like a good feature. The divorce rate is pretty staggering now – something like three in five couples, I understand.'

'Yes. Are you married?'

'No, more's the pity. So what's your starting point? Ten years? Five years?'

'April 1975.'

'Why twelve years?'

The bar was almost empty and the two women sitting three tables away couldn't hear our conversation. Even so, I lowered my voice.

'It's not a divorce feature, Martin. The Deathmask killer is picking his victims from among women who got married in April 1975. We're trying to track them all down.'

'I see. But aren't the police doing that already?'

'I would imagine so, but they won't share their findings.'

'You could have problems,' he said. 'For a start, some of them will have moved since then. Others won't have bothered to register for voting so their names won't be included on the Register.'

'I know, but it's a start.'

We arranged to meet at his office at 10 a.m. the following morning and then he left for a dinner engagement. I didn't have a car so took a bus home. As it approached the hospital, I thought of Sue. My cats would be getting hungry, but I wanted to see her. The bus pulled away while I was considering my options and I got off at the next stop and walked back.

A light shower developed into a major downpour before I reached the sanctuary of the hospital entrance. Once inside, I dithered some more. I was soaking wet and wouldn't know what to say.

I found the gents toilet and dried myself off with paper towels, stopping before a mirror to comb my hair. The eyes that looked back at me were mocking and a cynical smile hovered at the mouth. Once again, I saw Jeremy Miller as others saw him. *I* knew the eyes were frightened, the mouth twisted in nervousness. But then I was inside the fortress looking out.

I went to the ward and found she'd been moved. A young nurse directed me to her floor and I discovered Sue was now in a long ward with some two dozen other women. I looked through the round porthole window in the rubber doors and saw Phil Deedes by her bed, holding a bunch of flowers.

I was about to go home when Deedes stood to leave. I moved away from the door and wandered down the corridor past the lifts. I chose a vantage point near a pillar and waited until Deedes had gone, then made my way back to the ward. Sue's eyes were closed as I approached the bed and I stood silently for a moment, gazing down at her. Her honey-blonde hair was now showing darker roots, and her face looked younger without make-up. The surgeons had done a good job on the gash to her forehead and there would only be a faint scar.

'Hello, Jeremy,' she said, jerking me back to the present.

'Hi. How are you feeling?'

'Not bad. Sit down.'

I scraped a chair across the floor, feeling clumsy, and sat on her left.

'You're lucky to be alive.'

'I know, but I don't feel very lucky at the moment. How's work?'

'Everybody misses you. Especially Don.'

'Sweet man. He comes here every night. You missed him by about ten minutes. He told me you brought a faith healer here.'

'Yes. It couldn't do any harm, could it?'

'No. Would you pour me a glass of orange juice?'

I did so and then helped her to sit. It was the first time I'd ever touched her while she was conscious. I noticed then that her left arm was flopping alongside her.

'Is there any improvement in the hand yet?' I asked.

'Sometimes it tingles, and the fingers jerk by themselves. They say the feeling will come back. Tell me about this faith healer.'

'Don says that when you came to, you asked about him, as if he reached right down into your mind.'

'I know,' she said. 'It's so galling not to be able to remember. How did you meet him?'

I told her about Mr Sutcliffe and Ethel, and then about my cats, and my flat, and my life. In short, I probably bored her ears off.

At last, I noticed how tired she looked and stammered an apology.

She smiled then. 'I think I will sleep now. Thanks for coming, Jeremy.'

'Call me Jem. Most of my friends do – or they would if I had any friends. I'm not very good at making them. I'm sorry for the way I was to you.'

'Goodnight, Jem.' Her eyes closed. Knowing she had no feeling in her left hand, I reached down and gently squeezed the fingers.

19

Mark Fletcher stubbed out his cigarette and sipped his cold coffee. He had been on the Force for eighteen years, through two failed marriages and a crippling car accident that left him in permanent pain from a twisted spine. In all that time, he'd never lost his love for police work, or to be more precise, detective work. As he constantly told the officers under him, the word said it all. Detective. Detecting the subtleties, seeing the rhythms, hooking on to the invisible lines that linked all clues.

Fletcher was a genius. He knew it, his subordinates knew it, and his superiors knew it. It made him extremely unpopular.

He sat now at his cluttered desk, staring down at the files and jotting notes on a large pad.

The first words were 'April 1975'. Not just important, but crucial. It was the only visible link between all the women. The killer was the invisible link. Most murders were committed within families by relatives, often husbands or wives. Crimes of passion. Sudden violence. Some were committed during the course of other crimes. This case was different. Here they were dealing with an intelligent psychopath who chose his victims with care.

Fletcher lit another cigarette, sucking the smoke deep into his lungs.

Barbara Sinclair had been the first victim. Why? Why not

Dorothy Bowyer or Agnes Veronia? What made Barbara Sinclair special? He opened her file. She was thirty-eight years old and a secretary. No known lovers, no known hobbies. The photograph of her face had been taken after death and the eyes had already sunk. Still, the face had been pretty enough. A former Faraday School girl whose English teacher remembered her as 'vivacious and fun-loving, talkative and bright'. Fletcher pulled the sheet on Gary Sinclair. Personnel manager at Watkins Industrial. They separated in 1984 after Sinclair discovered his wife had been 'seeing other men'. Fletcher grinned. *What a lovely old-fashioned phrase. She slept around. She screwed. She swallowed the sausage. Seeing other men? Jeez!*

He scanned the ex-husband's file. Sinclair was a member of the Vikings Pistol Club and had a license for three weapons, a Webley .38, a Colt Python .357, and a Browning Hi Power 9mm. Fletcher put his hands behind his head. He didn't like to make assumptions, but he felt he could see inside Sinclair's head. A man unable to satisfy his own wife but who messed around with guns. Phallic substitutes, perhaps, the weapons replacing his weary sex drive? There was a note from Adams attached to the file. A Dr Van de Teele had confirmed that Gary Sinclair was in hospital in Amsterdam the night Barbara Sinclair died. His bed had been checked three times during the night, as per hospital practice. So what were the options? He didn't kill her. Did he pay someone else to do it? Why? There was no insurance. And why wait three years?

Fletcher moved on to Dorothy Bowyer. A 41-year-old telephonist at the Banberry Trade Centre. Lovers: none. Hobbies: none. No children. Divorced eight years ago after husband Jack was caught out in an affair with a fellow teacher. 'They stayed friends.' Fletcher didn't believe that for a minute. He was friends with neither of his ex-wives. According to the report, Jack Bowyer was a physical-fitness addict, tall, strong and athletic. Options? He could have killed Barbara Sinclair to cover the murder of his own ex-wife. Why? Again no insurance. No motive.

Agnes Veronia, aged 35, West Indian and a prostitute. According to neighbours, she'd gone on the game eight months before, after her daughter Rebecca developed kidney disease. No space on a dialysis machine and Mrs Veronia was trying to get the money together to buy one. Then the daughter died but she'd fallen into bad ways and couldn't come back. Then Mrs Veronia attempts suicide, and is brought round only to be murdered. Ex-husband Milton now living in Jamaica. Lovers? Legion. Hobbies: none.

'You didn't have much luck, Agnes.'

He lit another cigarette while the stub of the last still smouldered in the ashtray, then stood and walked to the window. Somewhere out there was a young man, strong and fast, who had developed a hatred for a group of women whose only crime was to be divorced having married in April 1975.

He was tall and ambidextrous. He stitched the women using his right hand, but he killed Bealey with his left.

'I'll find you, you evil bastard,' Fletcher whispered.

I watched Martin and his magic computer for around half an hour. It was mind-numbingly dull, just a sequence of symbols and names flashing in green letters across a black screen. I began to wander around the office, admiring the elm-panelled walls and the oil paintings in their alcoves. They were all landscapes, and beautifully composed. I looked for signatures but none of them were signed. From the window, I could see the old cinema, which was now a

DIY warehouse. The ODEON letters were still on the side of the building and I remembered queuing for two hours to see Jaws chomp on a number of nubile Americans.

'Nearly there, Jeremy,' said Martin, without looking around from his screen. 'Go and ask Dorothy for a cup of coffee. I can feel your tension from here.'

Dorothy was past retirement age by some five years, but, according to Martin, was five times better than the modern comprehensive crop. She was short and stout with iron-grey hair that still showed a trace of blonde, and her voice could best be described as 'no-nonsense'. No one messed around near Dorothy Kepper.

She was typing furiously on a word processor when I entered her small office. She didn't look up. The coffee jug was full and there were spare cups, milk and sugar. I toyed with the idea of helping myself, and abandoned it.

'Yes?' said Dorothy, after a minute of uncomfortable silence broken only by the clatter of electronic keys.

'Martin asked me to get some coffee.'

'It's over there,' she said.

'Thanks. Would you like one?'

'I have mine at 12.15,' she answered, and the clatter began again.

Back in the elm-panelled office, I watched Martin type the word PRINT and six names and addresses appeared to his right, snaking across a single sheet of A4. He lifted it from the printer.

'Four of your couples have left the area. One's in Newcastle, one in Australia, two unknown. The rest are all still local.' He handed me the sheet. By the side of five of the addresses were telephone numbers.

'I don't know how to thank you,' I said. 'You've saved me days of work.'

'I enjoyed it. Man does not live by squash alone. Let me know how you get on.'

Back at the office, I took out my notebook and lifted the phone receiver. The first two women I called were still married and I crossed them off my list. The third was a widow; the fourth divorced. I asked if I could pop round to see her, citing once more the fictitious article. She said no.

'It's really very important, Mrs White.'

'Not to me. You newspaper lot spend all your time prying into other people's business. Well, I don't like it. Goodbye.' The line went dead. There was no reply from the last telephone number. At a loss, I went to see Bateman.

'You'll have to go round to their homes this evening,' he said.

'I've got to cover Environment Committee.'

'See if you can swap with Oliver. Tell him I asked it as a favour.'

'He doesn't like me, Don.'

'He's got good reason. You humiliated him publicly. Okay, I'll talk to him. You still in Coventry?'

'As good as.'

'It'll pass. Just keep working as hard as you have been. Andrew is very impressed with your recent work rate. So am I.'

'Thanks.'

That afternoon, I was scheduled to interview a vicar in the east of town about a fundraising drive for a new church roof but he wasn't there – his wife explained that he'd been called away to a sick parishioner. I made another appointment and walked to the car. From the street, I could see the newsagent's run by Dawn Green's parents. I wandered across the road and walked inside. Her mother wasn't behind the counter. Instead there was a short, tubby man with thick grey hair.

'I've come to see Dawn,' I said.

He smiled. 'You from the *Herald*?'

'Yes.'

'Are you the lad that wrote the piece?'

'Yes – was it okay?'

'It was lovely, son. I'll treasure that. There's someone with her, but you can just pop up there.'

The room was bright, with sunlight streaming through the open window. By her bedside sat a young West African kid in a black leather bomber jacket and jeans. I smiled at him, but it wasn't returned. He simply stood, said a fast goodbye to Dawn and walked by me.

'It's a lovely day,' I said, moving into her line of vision.

'It's the poet,' she answered, grinning.

'I'm no poet.'

'Your piece was full of poetry and romance.'

'Didn't you like it?'

'Of course I did, but it wasn't true, was it?'

'True? All your quotes were as you said them. I don't understand.'

'I'm not complaining, Jeremy. But you made me sound like some tragic princess who radiates love and understanding. I'm not. I'm a quadriplegic who doesn't even know when she's messed the bed. If by some miracle I was cured tomorrow, it wouldn't be long before I learned again how to be angry, or envious, or greedy.'

'I think you're too hard on yourself,' I told her. 'And the piece was true – at least for me.'

'That's because you're a romantic. And it's a lovely thing to be. How is Sue?'

'On the mend. There's some paralysis, but it will pass.' I could have cut my tongue out.

'I'm glad. She's a lovely girl, so full of life.'

'Who was the man here when I came in?'

'His name's Justin. He lives in Beech Close. He comes to see me a lot. He's just got a job at the big garage on the main road – he's going to be a mechanic. It's his first real chance. He left school two years ago and has been out of work since. He's a bit frightened at the thought of working.'

'How did you meet him?'

'He just came in one day. People do that, you know. It's very nice. He wanted to meet your tragic princess. He wanted to understand how anyone like me could see the world through the eyes of God.'

'And I'll bet he did, otherwise he wouldn't have come back.'

'You're a lovely boy, Jeremy. I like you a lot.'

'I like you, too,' I told her, amazed by how easy it was to say, as if my fortress walls had melted away. 'And call me Jem.'

'Jem. That's better. Jeremy is so formal and distant. I'm very tired now, Jem. I've had a lovely day, and I think I'll dream for a while. I still walk in my dreams, you know. And dance. And run.'

Her eyes closed and I sat with her as she dozed off, enjoying the tranquillity.

Her father came in, saw she was asleep and offered me a coffee. I joined him in the long lounge next door. He was a gentle man, soft and yet without weakness. We drank our coffee in comfortable silence and then I rose to leave.

'Thank you for coming,' he said, as if I'd bestowed some priceless gift on his home.

'It was a pleasure. I mean that. I'll see you soon.'

Dawn Green died that night. No one had expected it. I like to think she was dancing when it happened.

20

It's a terrible truth, but no one understands death until it reaches out and touches someone close; until you stand at a bedside staring at sunken eyes and total immobility.

'She looks very peaceful,' said Mrs Green in a half-whisper as we entered the room. I would rather have been anywhere else in that moment. The sun was beating against the drawn curtains, sneaking into the room in tiny slivers around her bed, like the beginnings of a web of light. But she didn't look peaceful. Or restful. Just dead.

Nothing moved. It may sound strange, but that was the real shock. If you look at a sleeping face, there is always movement, infinitesimal muscle twitches, the beating of a pulse in the neck. That's what they mean when they say peaceful. They don't mean tranquil, or beautiful, or at rest. They mean still.

'I'll leave you alone with her for a minute,' whispered Mrs Green. I didn't want to be alone. My Dawn had gone. But I moved to the bedside anyway, forcing myself to look down at her face. The blood had drained from her features, making her skin look like wax. I didn't take her hand. I couldn't.

I glanced around. Mrs Green had shut the door behind her.

'I am so sorry,' I said. The lump in my throat broke into a hundred angry pieces and the tears gathered behind my eyes, unstoppable. I dragged open the curtains, allowing the waiting sun to bathe her with life. It was probably a trick of the shadows, but she looked like she was smiling now.

I wished then that I could believe in a religion – any religion. I wanted to see her dancing and running into the arms of God, glorying in movement and strength that would last an eternity.

You're a lovely boy, Jeremy. I like you a lot.

I hadn't cried like I did then in all my life, heaving sobs I couldn't control, streaming tears that felt as if they'd flow without end. But even in that misery, Dawn gave me something. I could see the awful waste of my life and the little fears I'd built into spectacular terrors. My shadow-haunted fortress dissolved and, in a curious way, the sunlight appeared to move from Dawn's body to encompass me. I did take her hand then. It was stiff, but not as fearful as I had imagined. Slowly, the tears eased. I still couldn't speak to her. Every time I tried, the sobbing began again.

I remembered reading somewhere that for three days after death, the soul is flowing from the body in waves of invisible fire. I hadn't believed it, But it helped me to say my farewells.

When I stood and turned, I saw Andrew Evans behind me. But there was no embarrassment. He handed me a handkerchief and stepped forward. He, too, was tearful and I felt as close to him as a brother.

We journalists are a weird and wonderful bunch. Most people think we're cynics, because we mock and see through the posturings of politicians, the shallow greed of businessmen, and the many and varied faults and flaws of a material society. But we are not natural cynics. We enter journalism because of our ideals, marching in as romantics who think we can change the world.

But the more we experience, the more hardened the

exterior becomes, and that's all people see. Yet deep down, beneath the suit of steel, the romantic waits, full of hidden longing.

Andrew and I went out into the street and we both looked up at the window. But there was no face there now, looking down at the world. Mrs Green appeared and drew the curtains once more.

'It'll be a great front-page lead,' said Andrew.

'Yes.'

'You'd better write it. Fancy a drink?'

We walked in silence to the nearest pub and sat quietly in a corner. Neither of us wanted to talk about Dawn.

'What have you got planned for this afternoon?' he said.

'I'm off to see Mrs White.'

'I thought she'd refused an interview.'

'I'm going to see her anyway.'

'Okay. Phil's found two more divorcees in the bunch. We've passed the names and addresses to the police. They'll be watching them for a while.'

'I'm glad I met her,' I said, coming back to the subject on both our minds.

He had the good grace not to mention how I had argued against being sent round the first time.

What a lifetime ago that had been.

21

Mary was stretched out watching an old movie starring Richard Burton when the doorbell rang. It wasn't a good movie. Pressing the off switch on her remote, she swung her long legs from the sofa and walked to the door.

'Yes?' she asked the tall young man standing outside.

'Mrs White?'

'No, I'm the Queen of Sheba.'

'That was Gina Lollobrigida,' he said.

'What are you on about?'

'The movie. *Solomon and Sheba.*'

'Nice talking to you,' she said, swinging the door shut. The bell sounded again, as she knew it would, and she opened the door.

'Can we start again?' said the man.

'Make it interesting, because the next time the door shuts, it stays shut.'

'Three women have been murdered. All of them were married in April 1975 and subsequently divorced.'

She stood very still. 'Is this some sort of sick joke?'

'You know it isn't. My name is Jeremy Miller. I'm with the *Herald.*'

'You got a card or something?'

He fished in his leather jacket, coming up with a National Union of Journalists membership card.

'All right, you can come in.'

Mary knew the flat was untidy but clean. She lifted a pile of magazines from an old armchair. 'Sit there,' she told him as she resumed her place on the sofa. 'Now explain.'

As he told her about the murders, she found herself trying to place where she'd seen him before. He was a handsome boy, with intense eyes over high cheekbones. But she couldn't find the memory.

'I'm sorry,' she said, 'I missed that.'

He smiled, and she remembered!

'Chico!' she said, laughing.

'What?'

'You look just like that German actor in the *Magnificent Seven*. Horst something. He played Chico.'

'I haven't seen it,' said Jeremy Miller.

'Oh, you must have. Yul Brynner and six gunmen. It's a classic.'

'I don't like westerns much. Look, Mrs White, I'm trying to tell you about a murderer who might be hunting you.'

'Listen, love, I didn't know any of the women, but I bet they all had the same boyfriend, or they all went to Weight Watchers or some other group. Anyway, if a nutter came round here, my man would break his back. He's a weight-lifter.'

'Maybe so, Mrs White, but suppose I was the killer?'

Alarm swept through her. 'I think you'd better go.'

'All I mean is that your boyfriend isn't here all the time. Just tell me – and then I'll go – have you noticed anyone watching you lately, or had any strange phone calls? Anything unusual?'

'The only unusual thing is you turning up.'

The reporter stood. 'Thanks for your time, Mrs White. Just to be safe, we've passed your name on to the police, so if anything strange does happen, please ring them. Or if you're worried, ring me.'

'You'll find some other connection between them, I'm sure,' she told him as he walked to the door. 'You'll see. Nobody would kill people just because they were married in April 1975.'

'Here's my number. Please ring any time.'

As the door closed, Mary flipped the safety chain into place and went back to the film. Richard Burton and Roger Moore were talking and guns were blasting away in the background. She switched the set off and lit a cigarette. Anything with Roger Moore tended to lower her boredom threshold. The clock on the mantel shelf showed 3.15 and she wished Louis would come home early. She didn't enjoy sex with him, but it was better than watching television or being depressed by the news. Until she got cystitis. That was the trouble with Louis. Ram, bang! No finesse. All grunting and bruising. She giggled. Thinking about Louis screwing her was getting her aroused, yet the real thing left her cold and feeling somehow cheated. *Isn't life a bitch?* she thought.

She walked to the window.

'Come on, Louis,' she whispered.

At that moment, a board creaked in her bedroom. She swung around to see a black gloved hand on the door frame.

Outside in the street, I lit the first cigarette I'd had in days. I wanted to quit the revolting habit but didn't have the will-power. A car pulled alongside me, a silver-grey Jaguar. The window slid down smoothly.

'Hi, Jeremy.'

'Hello, Martin, what are you doing in this neighbourhood?'

'Well, I'm not cruising for a bruising,' he said. 'Hop in and I'll give you a lift.'

'I've got the company's Fiesta. What—'

Then I heard the scream.

'Call the police!' I shouted. I turned and raced back into the building and up the rickety stairs to the second-floor landing. I was way out of breath by the time I reached Mary White's door. I could hear the sounds of a struggle coming from inside. I hammered on the door with my fist, shouting at the top of my voice.

'It's the police! Open up!'

I heard Mary scream again and I threw my full weight against the door. It shuddered but didn't give. Something moved behind me. It was Martin Dunn.

'Help me!' I said. Together we crashed the door inwards. Lying on the floor was the blonde woman I'd just interviewed. Her red tracksuit top was now stained at the shoulder with deeper crimson. She tried to sit. I knelt by her, supporting her gently.

'I'll get an ambulance,' said Martin. He lifted the handset from a phone on the wall and dialled 999.

'What the hell's going on here?' boomed a voice. I looked around to see a huge black man standing in the doorway.

'Oh, Louis!' said Mary, bursting into tears.

'She's been attacked,' I said.

Louis knelt by her, then lifted her easily and carried her into the bedroom. I followed. The window was open. I went to it and looked down onto a flat roof fifteen feet below. The attacker was nowhere in sight.

'Who are you?' said Louis.

I told him, keeping my voice level. He looked on the verge of exploding and I didn't want him moving in my direction when the bang hit.

Martin brought a white towel from the bathroom and handed it to Louis. 'You should press this against the wound. The ambulance will be here soon. I'll make some tea. Sugar?' he asked Louis.

'Yeah. White with two. You all right, doll?'

Mary nodded. 'It was awful, Louis. I was watching TV, he came out of the bedroom. He was wearing a mask with the word DEATH on it. He had this long needle ...'

I left the room. 'Did you ask for the police, too?' I asked Martin.

'Sorry. I wasn't thinking. I just requested the ambulance. But I assume, when I said someone had been attacked ...'

I called Mark Fletcher's direct line and outlined the attack.

He was at the flat within twelve minutes, beating the ambulance by three. In that time, he spoke to Mary White alone.

The Scenes of Crime Officer, a burly ex-sergeant by the name of Don Dodds, arrived shortly afterwards and began dusting for prints around the windowsill. I went with Fletcher to his car.

'Lucky you were close by, Jeremy.'

'If I hadn't met Martin by chance, I'd have missed it.'

'How does it feel to be a hero?'

'What, for pretending to be a policeman? I'm lucky he ran, otherwise he'd have killed me. But Mrs White put up quite a struggle.'

'She did well. Nice-looking bird, too. What's the deal with your pal?'

'Martin? He's a local businessman. Computers. And he's the town's Good Samaritan.'

'I saw the Gieves and Hawkes jacket. I'd like to be able to afford one of those.'

'You'll have to up the charges for avoiding remand.'

'Don't even joke about that, son,' he snapped. 'I've never taken a backhander in my life, and I've been offered a few.'

'It was a bad joke. Sorry.'

'Bloody right!'

I was pictured on the front page of the next *Herald*, along with Mary White, Martin and Louis. I was a hero, and I have to say I enjoyed it immensely. Poor Dawn, whose story was scheduled to be the week's lead, was shoved back to page three.

The London evenings and the dailies had already carried the story of Mary's escape under various headlines. BLONDE FOILS DEATHMASK is the one that sticks in my mind, but only because the banner ran over the top of a Page Three girl with enormous breasts. I was quoted in the story carried by the *Daily Mail*. My mother kept the cutting in the leather-bound family scrapbook. It was all I could do to stop her framing it.

Local journalist Jeremy Milner pounded on the door and the killer fled. Mr Milner said later, 'I am glad I was able to help.'

I couldn't help but feel superior about their inability to spell my name correctly. What sort of journalism was that?

'Anyone been on to you yet about the film rights?' Andrew Evans asked the morning after the attack.

'Spielberg is flying in later this week,' I told him.

I was no longer in Coventry. Oliver Cappel made me a cup of coffee. Phil Deedes smiled and loaned me his sweeteners when the sugar ran out. God, it gave me a nice feeling. As did the *Herald* headline: OUR MAN SAVES VICTIM 4. Not as garish as *The Sun*, but I couldn't stop mother framing them both.

Everywhere I went, people congratulated me. I was loathsomely modest about the entire business. Much the same happened with Martin, who told me he'd never known such praise for running up some stairs and vandalising a door.

In the meantime, life went on. The murderer seemed to have been scared off for the moment. There was another near-riot on Lansdowne; the unemployment figures soared two hundred and seventeen per cent over the previous month; and August slid by in a succession of sunshine, gales, storms and thick cloud. Summer sneaked in and out on a hot Thursday then took a long break in the south of France without saying goodbye.

I spent a lot of evenings with Sue Cater at the hospital. The feeling came back slowly to her left hand and after more than a month in bed she was released one Tuesday evening at the end of summer. I picked her up in the new Editorial Fiesta and drove her home. Her flat was cold and dusty, and she leaned on me as I carried her bag into the lounge. There were more stairs than she remembered and her face was red, her breathing ragged. I sat her down in an armchair and lit the wall-mounted gas fire. From a carrier bag, I took a bottle of milk, a jar of coffee and a packet of sugar. Her kitchen was small and neat and I found two mugs in a wall unit. One had the name David around the middle. I carried the coffees through to the lounge.

'Who's David?'

'An old friend – an ex-friend,' she said. She took the mug in trembling hands and sipped the hot, sweet liquid.

'You look tired.'

'I am tired. And a bit afraid.'

I sat opposite her. 'Afraid of what?'

She shrugged. 'Being out. Starting life again. Being on my own.'

'How's the coffee?'

'It's fine. Am I embarrassing you, talking about this stuff?'

141

'Yes, but feel free. It's what friends are for. How long since you and David broke up?'

'Three days before the crash. He went back to his wife.'

'Oh. I see.'

'Don't be so prissy. *Oh. I see!*' she mimicked. 'You don't see at all.'

'I'll get a big stick and you can hit me with it.'

She chuckled. 'What do you think of my flat?'

I looked around. There were no pictures on the walls, which had been painted a soft pale green. The furniture was old but well made and re-covered in dark green cloth. In place of carpets, half a dozen rugs were scattered about the varnished wooden floor. It was a small lounge, but cosy.

'It's relaxing here.'

'Is that the best compliment you can think of?'

'Well, I haven't seen all of it yet.'

'There's not much else to see.'

'There's the bedroom,' I said. My face began to colour. I hadn't meant it as a sexual advance, but that's the way she took it. I could read it in her eyes. A stillness settled between us, raw and uncomfortable. I knew I was expected to say something else. She was waiting, and I was lost in a silent panic. Then the moment passed and I knew I had let a precious chance slip away.

'Thanks for bringing me home,' she said, in a pleasant goodbye voice.

I rose, trying to smile, battling to be smooth and easy, failing.

'I've never had a girlfriend,' I told her, 'so don't judge me too harshly if I'm not much good at speaking to women.'

'Jem!' she called as I reached the door.

'Yes?'

'Come back here. I don't want to be on my own.'

What else could I do? I went back and stood near her.

'Why don't you stay the night?' she asked. 'And that's not a sexual invitation. I'm not exactly feeling up to Shakespeare's beast with two backs.'

I reddened. 'I just made a terrible fool of myself.'

'No, you didn't,' she told me, 'and that's close to being a first for you.' She moved to the sofa. 'Come and sit by me.' I did as she asked. 'Now kiss me. Gently.'

I leaned over her, my lips brushing against hers, lingering long enough to feel her warmth. My knee touched hers. Then I returned for a longer kiss.

'Come to bed,' she said.

'I thought—'

'For a cuddle. To touch. To get to know.'

The bedroom was tiny, the double bed almost filling the entire space. Above it was a narrow light, to one side a small table with phone and a haphazard pile of books. I stripped off my clothes but kept my boxer shorts on. Sue slid into bed beside me and began removing clothes under the cover.

'I'm cold,' she said. I slipped my left arm under her head and curled my hand around her shoulder, drawing her to me. Beneath the sheets, I felt her left thigh rub against my right leg, and her hand stroking my chest and belly. She kissed my cheek, silently inviting me. I responded instantly, turning to her. My fingers roved over her skin.

'Take off those ridiculous shorts,' she whispered.

'They're the ones from the jeans ad,' I said. 'They're supposed to be all the rage.'

She chuckled and twanged the elastic. 'Take them off anyway.'

I wriggled clear of my underwear. 'I was—'

'And don't talk.'

Her hand slid down my belly and I closed my eyes, my

body tense. My fingers mirrored hers, drawn to her heat. I tried to manouevre myself on top of her.

'No,' she said, kissing me.

The phone rang by my ear. I swore. Leaning over me she swept up the receiver.

'Hello? Oh hi, Don. No, I'm fine. Jeremy brought me home. Yeah. The doctor signed me off for two more weeks of convalescence. Sure? That would be nice. Tomorrow? Okay. Yeah. Thanks for ringing.'

She left the receiver off the rest and cuddled up alongside me again. Her hand moved down. Gone was the erection. Throwing back the sheets, she kissed her way over my chest, my belly, my ...

'No!' I said. 'I thought you didn't...'

'Lie still, Jem.'

Her mouth moved over me and I groaned.

'Isn't that better?' she whispered, moments later.

I couldn't deny it.

22

Mr Sutcliffe slowly buttoned his green denim shirt, tucked it into his trousers and resumed his seat. The doctor was a small man in his middle thirties.

'Well?' said Mr Sutcliffe. 'Is it as you suspected?'

'You're as strong as an ox and quite the fittest man approaching seventy I have ever known. But yes, it is as I suspected – all the tests confirm the aneurism.'

'Can it be treated?'

'I'm afraid not. It's an erosion of the tissue around the heart – it's paper-thin and could rip at any time.'

'How long do I have?'

'It's not that simple, Mr Sutcliffe. I wish to God it were. You're a strong man, both physically and emotionally, so I won't sugar the pill. You could die outside this office a minute from now, or you could go on for perhaps a month, maybe two. But the heart will give way sooner or later. All I can suggest is that you avoid strain and get your affairs in order.'

'There was a time when I could run for a full day, carrying a pack. Even now my heartbeat is only forty-four. It is hard to believe that so powerful an organ will betray me.'

'I take it you've been blessed with good health all your life?'

'Free from disease, yes,' said Mr Sutcliffe.

'But not from hardship. Unless I miss my guess, those are old bullet scars in your lower back.'

'You are astute, Doctor. They are indeed.' He offered his huge hand to the GP and thanked him.

Outside in the gathering dusk under a grim, grey sky, the towering black man grinned. In three months he would have reached three score years and ten. He began to jog along by the Green, feeling the muscles tighten in his calves, his arms swinging rhythmically. His breathing deepened; his heart swelled. Slowly the houses slid by him until he'd run all the way across Lansdowne with its depressing towers, stopping a hundred yards short of his terraced house.

He could feel his heart pounding in his chest.

'This is life!' he whispered, exulting in the savage joy of victory. Then he smiled. Once, his victory had been in running down and killing a lion with his assegai. Years later, it had been escaping from the security forces with three bullets in his back. Now it was a half-mile jog through the backstreets of Lansdowne.

Oh, how time makes fools of us all, he thought.

A light was shining behind Ethel's lace curtains and he felt in need of company. He tapped at her door. She opened it and he noticed with only mild irritation that the safety chain was not on.

'The tea's just made,' she said. She was wearing a simple white cotton blouse and dark slacks, and he thought how pleasant it would have been to have known her twenty years ago. He followed her into the lounge and took his usual place in the far chair.

Yet would it have been so pleasant? Mangiwe Mazui had little love for whites then, as he scrambled through the bush country fighting a hopeless war. And Ethel Hurst was a married lady living in a London that had vanished for ever.

Mangiwe's mind floated back over the past two decades. He had been in Moscow … when? … twenty-two years ago this autumn. They had taught him to use the AK-47, to set up anti-personnel mines, to fire the rockets from the alloy tubes. They had even supplied him with three British passports. He still had one of them, though it had now expired.

He had come to London a year later to meet with two of the exiled leaders of his party. What a contrast he made, moving about in a sea of white faces, being stared at as an oddity, yet without rancour.

He recalled mentioning the lack of racism to Ezra as they sat in a small café near Hampstead Heath.

'Do not be fooled,' he had said. 'They have their hates, even as we do. They hate the Poles, and the Irish. But we are not a threat to them. And that is the greatest insult of all. We are the golliwogs, Mangiwe. We do not have the brains to think. We are the jungle bunnies. We eat missionaries and perform in Tarzan films.'

'And yet,' said Mangiwe, 'it is good to feel the absence of hate.'

'Give them time. They will learn.'

'Perhaps not. They are not like the Americans.'

Ezra had laughed then. Had he not been tortured to death in an underground security cell, he would be laughing still.

'You are miles away,' said Ethel.

'Centuries,' he said, smiling. 'Why do you stay here, Mrs Hurst? You have become like a foreigner in your own birthplace.'

'Nonsense. All things change, Mr Sutcliffe. I like this town and its people. They have always been friendly to me – and to poor Freddie when he was alive.'

'But the anger and the hatred—'

'It does not touch me. Old Mr Seymour was mugged

yesterday, but two men ran from their homes and chased away the youths. Both of those men were black. They helped Mr Seymour home. He lost his pension. But this morning an envelope was put through his door containing thirty pounds. What do you make of that?'

'What *should* I make of it? It was a fine gesture. But I am not saying that there are no good men and women among the community. I am only pointing out that you are now a foreigner here.'

'I do not accept that, either,' said Ethel. 'All those children playing in the yards and the backstreets are English. Your problem is that you have no sense of history. Once upon a time, the Belgae invaded this land. They were Celts, tall and blond, artistic, creative. A few hundred years later, the Romans invaded. Short, stocky, dark and speaking Latin, masters of organisation. There were many bloody wars and the two races hated one another at first, but they blended as the centuries passed. Then the Saxons, the Jutes, the Danes and the Angles all came and conquered, and after them the Normans. But they didn't really win. The land beat them all. It absorbed them, bred them and interbred them. That's why Britain conquered the world – because, like a mongrel dog, we're tougher than the pedigrees. Now drink your tea before it gets cold.'

'That was a powerful speech, Mrs Hurst,' he said, lifting his mug.

'I read a lot, Mr Sutcliffe. Now what did the doctor say?'

'He said I am as strong as an ox.'

'Truly?'

'Would I lie to you, Mrs Hurst?'

'I think you just did, Mr Sutcliffe,' she said sadly, lifting the tea cosy and feeling the pot.

'No one lives for ever, Ethel.'

'No, indeed not. What a terrible thing that would be. More tea?'

'Thank you. Are you going shopping today?'

'Yes. Will you come?'

'Only if you promise to buy me scones and clotted cream.'

'You'll get fat, Mr Sutcliffe.'

'Fatness is a sign of greatness among the Matabele and the Zulu. I would very much like to grow fat. Fat and idle.'

'What did he say?' She was staring down at the table, unable to look at him.

'I have less than a year,' he said. 'Now we will not speak of it again. To do so would waste the time we have. And believe me, I will not die of some small complaint of the heart.'

'I don't think life would be terribly tolerable if you weren't here.'

'Did you not think that when Freddie died?'

'Yes, but I was younger then. More able to cope.'

'Nothing is for ever. Not life, not love, not friendship. You told me to learn from my roses, because they would grow again. I say the same thing to you. When you smell a rose, you feel the glory of beauty. But were you to look at that flower and think that in a little while it will be only decaying petals, its glory would fade. Enjoy the now, Mrs Hurst.'

'You called me Ethel a little while ago. I rather liked that, you know.'

'I rather liked it, too. Now let us shop and eat scones.'

23

'If you don't mind the old cliché, Mr Sinclair, it's just routine,' said Detective Inspector Mark Fletcher as he stood outside Gary Sinclair's detached home. Detective Sergeant John Adams smiled encouragingly and Sinclair stepped aside, waving his arm and beckoning the two men inside.

'Shouldn't you be out catching the killer?'

'Indeed we are,' said Fletcher, moving through to the panelled lounge. He stopped before the oil paintings, admiring the brushwork, especially the distant, lowering sky of the first.

'Will this take long? I'm going out.'

'Not long, sir,' said Fletcher, turning. 'You mind if I smoke?'

'Not at all. I'll get you an ashtray.' Sinclair brought Fletcher a small white saucer from the kitchen and sat in a cane armchair by the window. The two policemen sat and Adams produced a notebook and pen.

'So,' said Fletcher, lighting a cigarette and drawing deeply, 'when did you last see your wife?'

'I can't remember exactly. Months ago. We bumped into each other in a supermarket. We only spoke for about a minute, and even then she got several insults in.'

'You didn't like her?' said Fletcher.

Sinclair smiled for the first time. 'I loathed her.'

'Enough to kill her?'

'You want the truth? Of course you do. The answer is yes. Easily enough to kill her. I've lost count of the number of times I've pictured her throat under my fingers.'

'And did you, sir?'

'Oh yes, Officer. I made this straw dummy I left in the hospital bed and chartered a private plane to fly me over the Channel. Then I parachuted down and landed on her roof. It was a tough operation to plan. The hardest part was getting the Martians to teleport me back to Amsterdam.'

'Very helpful, sir. Have many friends did she have?'

'None that I knew of.'

'What about when you were married?'

'Not close ones, no. We had family friends. Working colleagues and their wives. They came to dinner sometimes. Then there were bridge evenings, but Barbara hated bridge – probably because she could never understand it.'

'So no special friends?'

'Not for her. You see, women didn't like her much. They knew she was an alley cat, and they were suspicious of the way she looked at their men. And men? I don't think any of her ... her lovers? ... liked her. They certainly never stayed with her long.'

'An unhappy woman, then, sir?'

'Very. With a unique talent for sharing her unhappiness.'

'Did she like music?'

'Music? What the hell has that got to do with anything?'

'Did she like music, sir?'

'Er ... Dire Straits, Bob Dylan and ... oh yes, Leonard Cohen. You ever heard Leonard Cohen's music? He's like a funeral procession going through life gathering mourners.'

'And films? What sort of films did she like?'

'Weepies, mostly. And anything with Clint Eastwood in it. She raved about him. A real man! You know what I mean?

Real men don't eat quiche! That sort of mentality. Real men don't get jobs as personnel managers. Real men carry magnums in their underpants. Bang bloody bang.'

'Any places she liked to go?'

'Places? What do you mean?'

'Nightclubs, pubs, discos?'

'She loved them all, but I hated them. No, there was no special place while she was with me. She went rock climbing about a dozen times, but that was with one of her lovers. I didn't find out for months. Another Clint Eastwood look-alike.'

'Did you go to the funeral, sir?'

'No.'

'How do you keep fit?'

'God! Where are these questions leading? I play squash, I do a little gardening and I jog. When you sit behind a desk all day, you get out of condition. How do *you* keep fit?'

'I run after murderers, sir,' said Fletcher. 'Thank you for your time. I may need to see you again.'

'Fine, I suppose? I'll get some recipes handy in case you want to know about my diet.'

Back in the car, Fletcher lit another cigarette. Adams wound down his window.

'What do you think?' asked the senior man.

'Very touchy,' said Adams. 'Why did you ask about music and films?'

'The questions weren't important. Let's move. We're late for Bowyer.'

Jack Bowyer lived two miles from Sinclair in a mock-Georgian four-bedroomed house on a new estate. His children were upstairs in bed and his wife out on a hen night.

'You mind if I smoke, sir?' said Fletcher, pulling out a cigarette.

'Yes, I do.'

Fletcher was irritated, and fumbled to get the cigarette back into the pack.

'Anti-smoker, are you?'

'Not really. But if I came into your living room and asked if you'd mind me lighting a bonfire of old leaves on your carpet, I wonder what you'd say?'

'Point taken.'

'Have a seat.'

'Thanks.'

'Drink?'

'Scotch, if you have it, sir.'

'And you, Sergeant?'

'Something soft,' said Fletcher. 'He's driving.'

'Lemonade, sir,' said Adams.

Fletcher settled back into the deep armchair and gazed around the room. There were no prints or paintings on the walls, but several plaques and trophies were displayed on shelves and cabinets.

'All for sport?' he asked as Bowyer handed him his drink and sipped from his own.

'Yes.'

Fletcher sipped the whiskey. 'That's good. Single malt?'

'Yes. Recognise it?'

'Glenmorangie?'

'Bushmills Irish. You can't buy it here. I pop across to France every now and again, pick it up in the duty-free.'

'Very nice, sir.'

'I'm glad you like it. Now, can we get to the point of your visit?'

'Of course. Did Mrs Bowyer – that's the first Mrs Bowyer – have any special friends?'

'There was Hilary Evans. She saw a lot of her, especially

after Donald – Hilary's husband – died. They used to meet several times a week. Dorothy was the sort of person with shoulders made to cry on.'

'Sympathetic, you mean?'

'Exactly that. She was a lovely person.'

'You betrayed her, though.'

Bowyer flushed deep red. 'Brutally to the point, Inspector. And I can't deny it, can I?'

'No, sir. How did she take it? The betrayal, I mean?'

'Badly. She didn't deserve it.' Bowyer rose smoothly and refilled his own glass. 'I'm not into confession, Inspector, but I still feel badly about what I did to Dory. No excuses. I couldn't say, "My wife didn't understand me," or that she nagged, or that she gave me any cause to … as you say … betray her. I simply got my sexual highs outside the marriage and one day fell in love with someone else. Sad, but true. Now, how does that help you catch her killer?'

'Who knows, sir? Murder investigations are seldom straightforward. It's like having a huge mixing bowl. You throw all the facts in, stir them around and see how the cake turns out.'

'Well, I wish you'd get a bloody move on. He's still out there.'

'We'll get him, sir.'

'Like you got Jack the Ripper?'

'Bit before my time, Mr Bowyer. I see the furniture is reupholstered. Another talent of yours?'

'My wife. She's good at that sort of thing.'

'Use long needles, does she?'

'I expect so.'

'How long?'

'I have no idea, and I hesitate to ask where this is leading.'

'You ever thought about killing anyone, Mr Bowyer?'

155

'Yes, Inspector. Haven't you?'

'Yes, but I've never done it, sir.'

'You think I have?'

'Have you, Mr Bowyer?'

Bowyer drained his whiskey and stood. 'I think this interview just ended. You morons have no idea who's butchering those poor women, and now you're looking for a scapegoat. Well, it's not going to be me. I'll see you out.'

'Thank you for your time, sir. It's been most valuable. Can you tell me where to contact Hilary Evans?'

24

He sat in the living room, nursing a long glass of homemade lemonade and crushed ice, staring at Marry, who was lazing on the sofa reading Tolkien's *Lord of the Rings*.

'I wrote to him, you know,' he said.

'Wrote to who?'

'To Tolkien.'

'You never told me that,' said Marry.

'When I was about twelve. I wrote to his publisher and they sent the letter on. I got a reply about six weeks later. I still have it somewhere. He used to live in a place called Sandfield Road, Oxford. It was a nice letter.'

'What did he say?'

'He said, "I'm glad you enjoyed my books, and yes I am writing another at present. I am afraid there are no Hobbits in it, but I hope you will read it someday."'

'How sweet.' Marry put down the book. 'You're still frightened, aren't you?'

'Yes. They almost caught me. It was terrifying.'

'That was weeks ago! They don't have anything on us, or they'd have been here by now. You know what you have to do.'

'I can't!'

'Yes, you can.'

'I think I'm going mad.'

'Nonsense!' Marry's arms slid around his neck. 'You're

living life to the full. Think about the joy, the exultation, the arousal. Remember the first time, and how good it felt. How right it was.' Soft lips brushed against his neck. He pulled away.

'They know! I can feel it. I want to stop – just for a little while.'

'Not when we're so close,' hissed Marry. 'If we stop now, it will all have been for nothing. He must suffer. And he will. He must already be sweating that the police will find out. And they will.'

'You promise it'll be over then? I know that sounds weak, but I'm scared.'

'Of course it'll be over,' said Marry. 'Trust me.'

Marry walked to a cupboard by the window and produced the black mask.

'Tonight. You must do it tonight.'

'Oh God, Marry.'

'Then we'll have that little holiday.'

'You promise?'

'When have I ever lied to you? How could I? I love you.'

It was after midnight when the phone rang beside Jack Bowyer's bed. He grunted and grabbed for the receiver before the noise could wake his wife from her pill-induced sleep.

'Hello?'

He listened as the voice whispered the black secret he feared.

'What do you want?' he whispered. Then: 'I don't keep that much money in the house, for God's sake!' He cast a glance at Wendy, who was still sleeping soundly. 'I've got about two hundred.' The voice gave him instructions. He slipped from his bed and quietly dressed.

At the end of August I took Sue to meet my mother, and I have to admit to a certain amount of trepidation. The lunch passed in uneasy conversation, then the two women retired to the kitchen. I stood silently in the lounge doorway, straining to hear their conversation.

'You're the first girlfriend Jem has ever brought round for lunch,' said Mother, scrubbing a plate and rinsing it before passing it to Sue for drying. Sue smiled. It had been a traditional English Sunday roast, beef and potatoes and overcooked vegetables. I guessed she'd fought to finish the overfilled plate. 'Jem tells me you work together.'

'Yes.'

Mother was a tall woman, slightly round-shouldered, with a quick, nervous smile that echoed mine. Or should that be the other way round? Of course it should.

'He's a good boy,' she told Sue, 'but I've always worried about him.'

'Why?' replied Sue, stacking the dishes on the wide draining board.

'I don't know, really. He always seems so lonely, even as a boy. He doesn't talk much about what he feels. I think his father's death hit him terribly.'

'When did he die?'

'When Jem was fourteen. It was very sudden.'

'It must have been hard for you, too.'

'Yes. About a year later, I was in hospital myself with a heart condition. Jem came to see me every day. There was an elderly lady who used to live near us – she's dead now – and I cooked her meals and took them round every evening. Well, when I was in hospital, Jem would come home from school and cook her meals and take them round, and then visit me. He did that every day for two months.'

'That's nice.'

'He's a good boy. But I suppose all mothers say that, don't they?'

'I expect so.'

'Thanks for your help, dear. Would you like to see the garden?'

'I'd love to,' said Sue. I was sure she was lying. It was neatly laid out with a winding path among the shrubs which gave the garden the illusion of size. At the far end of the path was a weeping willow, around the base of which someone had carefully constructed a circular wooden seat. I moved into the kitchen and quietly opened a window. I could just about hear their conversation as they sat down.

'It's a lovely seat,' said Sue.

'Thank you.'

'You made it?'

'When Jem's father died, I joined all sorts of clubs and organisations. One offered a carpentry class. I can also service cars.'

'I didn't know you had a car.'

'I don't,' said Mother, 'but when I do, I'll be able to service it.'

Sue chuckled. 'Do you never get lonely?'

'Sometimes. I do have … a friend. We go out sometimes. He's a widower, a retired teacher. He's good company.'

'You've never thought of marrying again?'

'I'm fifty-four, dear, and rather set in my ways. I like my life the way it is.'

I saw Sue grin.

'Well, don't worry about me. I'm not a femme fatale here to ruin everything.'

'I didn't think for one minute you were, but you can't stop

a mother worrying about her only son. He's far too easily hurt.'

'Pain is a part of life, Mrs Miller.'

'Call me Aggie.'

'Aggie? Is that Agnes?'

'Agatha. Aggie is more friendly. And I know what pain is, Sue. Let's go in and have some coffee.'

'I like him a lot, Aggie, but I'm not ready for wedding bells.'

'I only married his father because I was pregnant,' said Aggie, 'but it didn't work out too badly.'

'Are you suggesting I get pregnant?'

I almost swore out loud.

'No,' said Aggie, with a wicked grin. 'Your hips are too thin, and you'd get dreadful stretch marks.'

I saw them start back and darted to the lounge, quickly switching on the TV and settling back on the sofa. When they entered, they both had the same look, as if they were part of some sinister sisterhood.

We finished our coffee, said our goodbyes. Mother told me to be a good boy, then winked at Sue.

'She can be a weird lady,' I said to Sue as we drove away.

'I like her. She's very fond of you.'

'So I would hope.'

'How pompous! So I would hope? Sometimes I think you're very Victorian.'

'Just conservative.'

'I hope that isn't reflected in your political views.'

'I don't vote Tory.'

'I'm glad to hear it.'

'I don't think they're right-wing enough.'

'I'd forgotten you're all for hanging muggers.'

We drove to Richmond Park and walked through the grass

and under the trees, watching the deer living 'in the wild'. High rises rose in the distance like the bars of a vast cage. I guess the deer didn't notice.

I was feeling unsettled. Our conversation during the drive had been heated. I knew Sue was the secretary of the local Labour Party, but I naïvely believed our political views were separate from our personal feelings for one another. I should have switched the subject before it got out of hand, but common sense has never been my strongest suit.

'What you don't realise, with all your right-wing crap,' she said, 'is that you're proposing the survival of the fittest.'

'I know that. It's worked in the animal kingdom since the dawn of time.'

'We're not animals.'

'Balls! That's where you lefties have really naffed things up. That's *exactly* what we are. The same urges, the same adrenal drives. I'll tell you what you are – you're a bloody hypocrite.' I was always good at the softer, more persuasive styles of argument.

'How dare you say that? I fight for what I believe in.'

'So would I, given half the chance. But there's hardly any point adding my ounce of disinfectant to the cesspool your Loony Left has created.'

'Would you care to explain that?'

'Sure. You start out by telling children they don't have to excel. You teach them at the speed of the slowest. Then you inform them they have a "right" to a job, whether or not they're qualified. And a "right" to a home. And a "right" to a colour telly. When the poor buggers find out that it's all a pile of bullshit, they get angry and turn on the rest of us. They mug, they rape, they burgle, they kill. But that's okay – they're just "expressing their anger at society's injustices". So we put them in prisons where they can play football and watch their favourite TV programmes in colour. And just so they won't feel too hard done by, we let them out in a few weeks. Unless they've killed somebody. Then we let them out in a few months. It's a joke. Just a sick joke.'

'I suppose it's escaped your notice that we've had a Tory government for the past eight years?' she said.

'As I said, they're not right-wing enough.'

'I'm surprised we haven't got on to kicking the blacks out yet. Or chopping off shoplifters' right hands. Or scrapping the dole.'

'The world's gone mad,' I said, my anger ebbing away. I could never understand why people couldn't see that I was right.

'Take me home.'

'But it's a beautiful afternoon.'

'It was, but I'm not in the habit of spending my time with fascists.'

'Then get a bus!' I said and walked to the *Herald*'s car. It was locked.

And Sue had the keys.

I stood there as she drove away, my feelings indescribable, my desolation total.

25

Mark Fletcher kept his anger firmly under control as the bodies were carried from the flat. John Adams approached him warily.

'What's the score?' asked the detective inspector, lighting a cigarette and watching as the covered stretcher disappeared into the hallway.

'The boyfriend was killed as he slept,' said Adams. 'Then the woman was dragged into the living room and raped, then murdered with a long, thin needle-type weapon. You saw the stitching?'

'Of course I saw the bloody stitching. What I want to know is, where were the men who were supposed to be watching this house?'

'They were called to a domestic two streets away.'

'And what did they find?'

'It was over when they got there.'

'Over? I take it they checked out the address they'd been given?'

'I don't know, sir. I'll find out.'

'Pound to a bent penny there was no disturbance. How did he get in?'

'No sign of a break-in,' said Adams. 'All the windows are locked from the inside. The safety chain wasn't on the front door – mind you, a spade his size wouldn't think he needed one, I suppose.'

'I don't like the word spade, Adams. Or paddy, mick, wog, jungle bunny, frog or dago. Does that about cover it?'

'Yes, sir.'

'It demeans the user. And we've enough trouble in Landsowne already without officers using the jargon.'

'I'm sorry, sir.'

'You know what the papers'll make of this? We're going to look bad. Very, very bad. Mrs White survives one attack, only to be murdered while two police officers are on watch.'

'They were called away. It's not their fault.'

'What we're going to find, Sergeant, is that it wasn't anybody's fault. It'll be "just one of those things". We'll hear about undermanning, crossed wires, bad communication, and it all means the same thing. A young woman we knew was in danger was butchered by a maniac under our bloody noses. Get the deodorant ready, son, because the manure just hit the whirly thing, and we're about to be up to our necks in it.'

'Looking forward to it, sir. I've got the door-to-door going. A neighbour saw a blue car parked under a street lamp at about the right time.'

'What about the registration number?' asked Fletcher.

'C-reg. Had a six in it,' said Adams, 'and maybe an eight or a three.'

'Was there a driver inside?'

'Yes. Fair-haired. He didn't get out of the car while she was looking.'

'It's something, I suppose.'

'It's slightly better than that, sir. She said it was a Ford Sierra.'

Fletcher pulled a cigarette from his pack and stopped. 'One of our ex-husbands has a Sierra, doesn't he?'

'Yes, sir.'

Hilary Evans was a slender, bird-boned woman. Fletcher guessed her age at around forty. She lived in a small detached house in Ealing, on a tree-lined avenue that reminded the policeman of the Edgar Wallace mysteries of his childhood.

'Please come in,' she said, removing her horn-rimmed glasses and allowing them to hang on a long gold chain. The house was neat and clean, the lounge tiny and ordered, as if the chairs had been positioned using a set square to establish the perfect line.

'Do you mind if I smoke?' asked Fletcher.

'Do you mind if I break wind?' she answered sternly.

He dropped the pack into his jacket pocket. Adams was holding back a grin where he thought Fletcher couldn't see it.

'We'd like to talk about Dorothy Bowyer.'

'Yes. Poor Dory. What can I tell you?'

'When did you last see her?'

'About a week before she died. She came here for tea on Mondays. She sat right where you're sitting now.'

'What did you talk about?'

'I can't really remember. We used to chat about all sorts of things. Fashion, weather, politics, life.'

'What were her politics?'

'Left of centre. She liked people.'

'Was she happy?'

'I am not entirely sure what that means, Inspector. The English language is rarely exact. She was not depressed, but she was lonely. She never got over that … her husband leaving her.'

'You changed your mind about what you were going to say there.'

'I was going to say "swine". Which is what he is. She

167

deserved something so much better than him. But then, life is not about what you deserve, but what you get. Isn't that right?'

'I guess it is,' said Fletcher. 'But what makes you say he's a swine? A lot of marriages break up.'

'He could never keep his hands off other women. I think he was always trying to prove something. What's the phrase they use now? Macho. He made a pass at me once, about two months after my husband died. I had the satisfaction of telling him that twenty years of cordon bleu had left me no appetite for a shrimp-paste sandwich.'

Fletcher grinned. 'And what was his reaction?'

'He just walked away. Wouldn't you?'

'I rather think I would, Mrs Evans. Did you tell Mrs Bowyer?'

'No.'

'Isn't that rather odd? After all, you were friends.'

'I don't believe in destroying people for the sake of friendship. But even putting that high-flown moral view aside, I wouldn't have risked our friendship by telling her.'

'Risked in what way?'

'Are you divorced, Inspector?'

'Yes.'

'Was your wife unfaithful?'

'Yes.'

'How did you find out?'

'A friend told me.'

'Do you still see that friend?'

'I take your point, Mrs Evans. You should have been a policewoman.'

'I was a headmistress, Inspector, and these days it's much the same thing.'

'How did Mrs Bowyer get on with her ex-husband?'

'Very well. She still loved him, and in his own way he liked her. He used to see her once a week to brag about his achievements. Jack Bowyer is a man who needs to brag. You've visited his home? Have you ever seen so many trophies so prominently displayed? He climbed a mountain in North Wales once with a group of children and had special medals struck commemorating the event. You'll probably find he stills wears his under his vest.'

'Did Mrs Bowyer have any enemies? Did she mention receiving strange phone calls, anything like that?'

'No …' Hilary Evans hesitated. 'About a month before she died, she thought she was being followed. But she joked about it. I did think about calling your lot when she was murdered, but she always said it was nothing to worry about.'

'Perhaps you should have. What made her think she was being followed?'

'She said she kept seeing the same car parked near hers, and once, when she went into town by bus, it was right behind them all the way.'

'What kind of car?'

'She said it was blue.'

'And the make?'

'I don't remember her mentioning it. She said it was big, expensive-looking.'

'And the driver?'

'She said didn't see his face. You think it might have been the killer?'

'Perhaps, Mrs Evans.'

'I heard on the news that the murderer finally killed that poor woman he attacked.'

'I am afraid that's the case.'

'It hardly fills one with confidence concerning the ability of our police to protect us.'

'No. But we do our best, Mrs Evans.'

'Not good enough, Inspector. That phrase has been the clarion call of the incompetent for the last twenty years.'

'Thank you for your time, Mrs Evans. If you remember anything more about the car, please call me.' He handed her a card.

On the short driveway, Fletcher lit a cigarette and drew the smoke deep into his lungs.

'I've got to give this up,' he told Adams. 'I could barely think in there.'

'The desk sergeant gave up,' said Adams. 'He used hypnotherapy and acupuncture.'

'Frank Anderson?'

'Yes.'

'Has it done anything for his breath?'

'No. Still lethal from twenty yards.'

'There's something horribly wrong with that man's stomach.'

Adams climbed into the car and started the engine. Fletcher settled beside him.

'Where to, sir?'

'Back to the nick. I want to look at those files again.'

26

Mary White had been murdered in the early hours of the last day of August, and I wrote some three pages in my diary in a fruitless attempt to exorcise the fury I felt. I had saved that woman, and in a strange way, that made me feel responsible for her. Now my actions had proved worthless. My moment of greatness had been sullied and destroyed. For the first time, I felt a personal hatred for the killer. For the first time, he had invaded my life, reaching a ghostly hand into my memories and crushing a moment of self-worth.

Naturally, the press had a field day flaying the police and angry questions were asked in the House of Commons. As far as I could make out, the women in West London were being killed because of an uncaring government and public-expenditure cuts.

Wonderfully risible stuff. 'Here's another ten pounds, Inspector. Now find the murderer!'

The Home Secretary announced an internal inquiry, which is official jargon for 'doing as little as possible and hoping the problem will go away'. He also expressed his deepest sympathy for the relatives of the slain and called the killings 'the most monstrous crimes' in recent British history.

Poor Mary White. Poor Louis.

I remember reading once about a man who survived an airliner crash. He was sitting on the toilet at the time and the cubicle was thrown sixty feet from the plane. Everyone else was killed. He had a bruised ankle and a headache. Three days later, he had a coronary and died. I wondered then whether some celestial mistake had been made, that his time had been up on the plane but the angel in charge of collections had forgotten to check the lavatory.

But Mary? It would have been less terrifying for her if he'd succeeded the first time. What must she have thought as he woke her on his second visit?

Rascal leapt into my lap, thankfully disturbing my thoughts. I scratched at his ears. It had been three days since the Richmond Park fiasco, and Sue had barely said a civil word to me. She wouldn't let me in to her flat, or come out with me for a coffee and a talk. I tried to stay cool about it, but it was hard.

I shouldn't have sounded off as I did, but I believed everything I'd said.

What kind of a world were we living in? Pensioners were being called 'crumblies' because when you hit them, they broke. Women were unable to take a walk at night without fear of mugging or rape. Burglaries and assaults were increasing at a rate of forty per cent a year. The changes even in the ten years since I was a child were terrifying. West London was like a body covered in weeping sores. The Left said it should be put to bed and treated with tender loving care; the Right maintained it should be covered in disinfectant and the cancer cut out.

But people like me just lived in the middle of it, watching the disease grow and wondering where it would lead.

I tell you, that's where it's hard being a local journalist. You get to interview all the elements – the police, social workers, churchmen, councillors, dissidents, rebels and 'ordinary' folk. They all have differing views, and most are plausible.

Looking back through my cuttings book, I found an interview I'd conducted with a vicar called Richard Jones. Talking about muggers and inner city unrest, he said: 'The fundamental problem is one of self-worth. When we look in a mirror, we need to be proud of what we see. Not a vain, arrogant sort of pride, just a warm glow that we're worth something in the world, to our families, our workplaces, our society. Take that away and you have anger, resentment, even hatred. Without self-worth, a man has nothing. Nor will he appreciate the values of others.'

That was why I now felt such a personal loathing for the killer. My self-worth had increased following the rescue of Mary White. For the first time in my life, I felt I'd achieved something of real value. Mary White lived and breathed because Jeremy Miller had responded to a call for help. Every moment of joy she would experience, every smile, every second of happiness, was a gift from me. And now she was dead. Raped, murdered and mutilated.

I hoped the killer would burn for eternity in a very special kind of hell.

Alone with my anger, my thoughts whirled from Mary to Sue to Dawn Green, accompanied by a montage of emotions ranging from despair, through love and hate, and finally a deep melancholy.

The doorbell rang and I ignored it. It rang again. I walked to the window but couldn't see the figure in the shadows below. I opened the window and waited for the intruder to walk away.

When she did, I saw it was Ethel Hurst and called out to her.

'You must have been dreaming,' said Ethel as she removed her beige topcoat and looked in vain for a hook on which to hang it. I relieved her of it and draped it across the back of a chair.

'Can I offer you a coffee?'

'Tea if you have it, dear.'

'I'm afraid I don't.'

'Then weak coffee, please.'

I had no cups and the QPR mug looked out of place in Ethel's small hands.

'How are you, Jeremy?'

'Pretty well, thanks.'

She smiled softly and leaned back in the armchair. She was wearing a lilac sweater, black slacks and Hi-Tec trainers.

'Have you been running?' I asked her.

'No, but they are so comfortable and they ease my varicose veins. This is a nice flat. A little untidy, but nice.'

'I'm not terribly house-proud.'

'So I gather. You haven't been to see me for some time.'

'No. Life is very busy. You read about Mary? The murder?'

'Yes. It makes one feel so useless. A policeman named Fletcher came to see me. He was there the last time, you know, at the superintendent's office.'

'Were you able to help?'

'Not really. It's so frustrating, watching the killer, seeing his evil, and being unable to catch him. Mr Sutcliffe says he will eventually come after me. That's not a pleasant thought, Jeremy.'

'I think Mr Sutcliffe can handle him, Ethel. He looks like he could handle a Russian tank division.'

'Looks aren't everything,' she said, sadly. 'Mr Sutcliffe is dying. He has a heart complaint and I don't think he will see the new year.' She swung her head sharply and stared at the window, blinking back the tears.

'I'm sorry, Ethel. Truly.' They were just words, but I meant them as sincerely as anything I had ever said.

She looked back at me and smiled. 'It's life, I suppose. Nothing is for ever. Not even love.'

'Better to have experienced it, though,' I said.

'I sometimes wonder about that, Jeremy. All gifts are double-edged. Happiness is always transitory, like the seasons. I never really loved Freddie. We were happy, after our own fashion, but we never had that depth of love I dreamed about. When he died, I was distraught, but I coped. A friend of mine – Marsha – had a love like I always wanted. When she became a widow, she faded to nothing and died within six months. I suppose it is a form of balance, opposite sides of a coin – the greater the happiness, the more savage the sorrow. Which would you choose?'

'I don't know, Ethel. I've never been in love.'

'I'd swap with Marsha,' she said.

'Do you love Mr Sutcliffe?'

'Silly question. And I must go.'

'I'll drive you home.'

'That's not necessary.'

'No, but I will anyway.'

'You're a nice boy, Jeremy. You remind me of Bobby Ewing in *Dallas*.'

'I don't have a television, but didn't he die or something?'

'They brought him back. It was all a dream.'

I shook my head and grinned. 'How can you watch such rubbish?'

'Because it's better than real life, I suppose. Isn't that a sobering thought?'

27

Mark Fletcher knew he was missing something. Spread on the pine table before him were the thousands of words that made up the many reports and observations concerning the four murdered women, plus background information on the suspects.

He stared down at his notepad. The words 'Blue Car' were written there, followed by three large question marks. Now two of the suspects had blue cars. Sinclair had a silver Orion Ghia, Bowyer a blue Sierra, and the new man, Harry Cattlin, a blue Granada. Bowyer's registration was C263 SDY, and Cattlin's C816 SNJ.

Cattlin was Mary White's first husband, a mechanic now living and working in Hammersmith. The second husband was dead. Fletcher had seen Cattlin late the previous evening at his flat off the Fulham Palace Road. The man was over six feet tall, wide-shouldered and athletic, younger-looking than his forty-three years.

'Not much I can do to help you,' he said as Fletcher and Adams stood in the doorway.

'Can we come in?' asked Adams.

'I don't see why you need to. Just ask your questions and then push off.'

'Fine,' said Fletcher. 'We'll go now and come back with a warrant and about a dozen officers, and then we'll rip your pigging place apart. How does that sound, arsehole?'

'Come in, why don't you?' said Cattlin, stepping aside.

The flat was small and neat, the living room dominated by weight-training equipment.

'When did you last see Mary?'

'About ten days ago. She was with her new bloke, feeding the swans in the park. I said hello. That was about it.'

'You stay on friendly terms?'

'No. For two pins, I'd have wrung her neck years ago.'

'Ugly divorce, was it?'

'About as ugly as the marriage. I tried to give her everything she wanted. I took two jobs so she could have a foreign holiday. Wasn't good enough, though. Then she got pregnant. My baby! Had a bastard abortion, didn't she? I'll never forgive her for that.'

'Did you kill her?'

'No. And I haven't got an alibi, either. I stay in nights and work with my weights.'

'What about Agnes?' asked Fletcher.

'Never knew her.'

'You know who I mean, though.'

'I read the papers.'

'It's still unusual, Mr Cattlin. I only said her first name.'

'You really want to pin this on me, don't you? Well, go ahead and try. I don't give a toss.' He moved to the laminated dresser, picked up a newspaper cutting and dropped it into Fletcher's hand. 'I was reading this before you came. It's got a picture of Mary on it with all the other poor cows.' He slumped back into his chair. 'I could have wrung her neck, you know. But I didn't. Because I loved her. She was everything to me. And when she walked out, it was like somebody just turned off the lights and said, "Well, Harry, that's your life done." Can you understand that?'

'Can't say as I can,' said Fletcher, although he knew he

was lying to Cattlin. They'd ended the interview shortly after.

Now, back in his own flat, Fletcher sipped his coffee and scanned the notes once more.

A killer in a blue car who followed his victims in the daytime. Yet Sinclair, Bowyer and Cattlin all had jobs.

Easy answer? None of them was the killer.

But how likely was it that a maniac would go back to a newspaper cutting twelve years old to pick his victims? A car horn sounded from the street. Fletcher stubbed out his cigarette, gathered up his papers and joined Adams at the car.

'Morning, sir. Another nice day.'

Fletcher glanced at the clear blue sky. 'Lovely. Anything more on the cars?'

'There are several large blue cars at Watkins Industrial that Sinclair could have borrowed, but they would've been logged out to him and none of them were.'

At the station, Fletcher studied the notes for another hour, then filed them away.

Come on, Fletcher! You're supposed to be some sort of bloody genius. Think!

It didn't help that the press were stirring up a wave of panic with nonstop stories headlined WOMEN IN FEAR or WHO'S NEXT?, together with artists' impressions of hooded killers and photographs of long, wicked-looking needles.

The Home Secretary had promised action, but all that did was increase the burden on the men trying to do the job.

The two officers on duty outside Mary White's flat had been publicly pilloried. A cartoon published in a national newspaper showed two policemen outside a house which was being burgled by a number of masked men. One policeman was saying to the other, 'Look over there! It's a litterbug. Let's nab him!'

Yet the officers in question had done nothing wrong. They were on duty and responded to an order from Control. Fletcher had spoken to both of the men, but he could see from their eyes that his words were meaningless. They would carry Mary White's death with them like a sack of sins.

At 4.17 p.m. that afternoon, after a fruitless day, Adams entered Fletcher's office. 'Better take a look at this, sir.' He handed the inspector a single sheet of paper. On it were the words *Jack Bowyer is Deathmask.*

'This is a photocopy, sir. The original's being checked for prints. Typewriter is an Olivetti using Pica, forensics think. Machine is about three years old and needs cleaning.'

'What about the envelope?'

'Local postmark. Addressed to Mr Morris.'

'And the paper?'

'Canon photocopying paper.'

'From an office, then. Okay. Let's get going.'

At 6.35 p.m., armed with a warrant, Fletcher, Adams and four uniformed officers arrived at Bowyer's detached house. His wife Wendy let them in. She was a tall woman, fine-boned, what Regency writers would describe as handsome. Bowyer himself was in the bath. He came down to the lounge dressed in a white terrycloth robe.

'What the hell is going on here?'

'We have a warrant to search these premises,' said Fletcher.

'On what grounds?'

'Would you like to read the warrant, sir?'

Bowyer's oldest boy, a lad of around eight, peered round the door, his eyes wide.

'Better take him up to his room, Mrs Bowyer,' said Fletcher. 'Don't want him being upset, do we?'

As she left the lounge, Bowyer shut the door behind her. 'I don't understand,' he said, his face grey.

'Don't worry about it, sir. It'll probably come to nothing,' said Fletcher, pulling a cigarette from his pack and lighting it. 'Start in here,' he told the officers.

'But why?' repeated Bowyer.

'Why what, sir? Why didn't you mention your affair with Mrs Sinclair?'

'Jesus!' whispered Bowyer, sinking into a chair, his face in his hands. He looked up. 'That doesn't mean I killed her, for God's sake.'

'Sir!' said an officer standing beside a tall wall unit. Fletcher joined him. Pushed behind the laminated unit was a brown carrier bag. Fletcher reached in and drew it out. Inside was a black hooded mask and a long upholstery needle wedged into a cork.

'That's not mine!' screamed Bowyer, lurching from the chair, his eyes wide.

'Calm down, Mr Bowyer,' said Fletcher, softly.

'You brought that with you, you bastard!' Bowyer leapt at Fletcher, one fist swinging.

Fletcher ducked and jumped back as three officers moved in, grabbing Bowyer and wrestling him to the floor. The door opened.

'What on earth do you think you're doing?' shouted Wendy Bowyer.

'Take him upstairs and let him get dressed,' Fletcher said to two of the officers. 'Stay with him.' He turned to Mrs Bowyer. 'I'm sorry, madam, but your husband became violent. I'm afraid he's going to have to accompany us to the station.'

'This is insane,' she said. Then she saw the mask lying on the carpet and her hand flew to her mouth.

Bowyer was crying now and Fletcher knelt beside him.

'Your kids are upstairs, Mr Bowyer, so get a hold of yourself.'

'I didn't do it!'

'We'll talk at the station.'

Leaving two officers to continue the search, Fletcher joined Adams in the driveway.

'How did you know about his affair with Mrs Sinclair?' asked Adams.

'Rock climbing. You remember Sinclair talking about his wife going climbing with some Clint Eastwood lookalike? And then Hilary Evans talking about Bowyer climbing in Wales?'

'Even so, sir, a lot of people climb. It didn't have to be Bowyer.'

'No, but it was.'

'Well, this'll take the pressure off.'

'Don't be too sure, son.'

Bowyer was allowed to dress and then taken to one of the police cars, his hands cuffed behind him. Fletcher and Adams watched the car drive away and returned to the house. Wendy Bowyer was sitting on the sofa, her face grey with shock.

'I'm sorry, madam.'

'Dear God, it couldn't be him. It couldn't!'

Fletcher sat down beside her. 'It doesn't look good, does it? Did he go out on the night of the 31st?'

'No, I don't think so.'

'You don't think so?'

'I take sleeping pills. He's been very edgy lately, but I can't believe he'd kill women in that way. His trouble's always been that he likes women too much.'

'He certainly liked Barbara Sinclair.'

'She was just a whore,' said Wendy Bowyer, without a hint of malice.

'You knew, then?'

'She rang me. I think she expected me to have a blue fit and throw Jack out. I told her not to be silly and rang off. I didn't even mention it to Jack.'

'That's very understanding of you, Mrs Bowyer,' said Fletcher.

She smiled. 'That's how I got him in the first place, Inspector. By being understanding.'

'Has he ever struck you, or been violent in any way?'

'Never! It's not his nature. Do you really think he did it?'

'I'm afraid the evidence rather points to his guilt. But if he didn't do it, he won't be fitted-up for it. You can trust me on that. Either way, there's a team of officers heading over here who'll be going through the house with a fine-tooth comb. You understand the necessity?'

'Yes,' she said, wearily. 'I understand.'

'Tell me one thing, Mrs Bowyer. Are you happy with your husband?'

'I don't love him any more,' she admitted. 'And he has been a swine. But we're still friends. Always will be. Even after this.'

28

Bowyer sat in the main interrogation room, surrounded by four bare walls and staring at a tall uniformed officer standing by the door.

'I didn't do it, you know,' said Bowyer.

'No, sir,' answered the man, not looking at him.

'What's your name?'

'You just sit there quietly, sir. DI Fletcher will be along to see you in a while.'

'I only asked your name, for God's sake! It's not an official secret is it?'

'No, it's not, sir. Now just sit quietly.'

'Do you have any idea what this is like?' persisted Bowyer, his voice shaking. 'I haven't done anything wrong, and yet there's a bloody mask and a needle at my house. It's like a nightmare.'

Constable Gordon Riley knew exactly what it was like. Guilty or innocent, Bowyer was a lonely animal caught in a trap. The only other human being in his life at that moment was Riley, and the suspect was trying to make a friend of him. Riley enjoyed his Psychology courses. And the techniques had certainly helped him when it came to making friends of the opposite sex.

The door opened and DI Fletcher entered, followed by DS Adams. Fletcher sat opposite Bowyer and lit a cigarette.

Adams produced a notebook. He nodded at Riley, who did the same.

'Tell me about the mask, Mr Bowyer,' said Fletcher.

'What can I tell you? I've never seen it before.' Bowyer suddenly chuckled, although it had an edge of fear. 'What a cliché, eh?'

'Sounds like it, sir.'

'I suppose most clichés are truisms. I didn't kill Barbara – or Dory – or anyone else. And I can't begin to understand why the mask was there.'

'Perhaps you have enemies, sir.'

'Not that I know of.'

'Where did you meet Barbara Sinclair?'

'It was at a party at the school. She was dating the science teacher – George Phillips. They arrived late, and George was a little the worse for wear. Not drink, he had a dreadful headache. I offered to take Barbara home.'

'And then?'

'She was a very sexy lady, Mr Fletcher. We went straight to bed.'

'When was this?'

'About six ... seven ... months ago.'

'And after that?'

'I took her rock climbing in Kent several times. She was good company. A little self-obsessed, but witty.'

'When did you stop seeing her?'

'About three weeks before she was killed. She was getting heavy ... you know.'

'Assume I don't.'

'She was looking for a more permanent arrangement. It wasn't what I wanted.'

'What *did* you want, Mr Bowyer?'

'A little fun, and a little good company.'

'Did you argue?'

'Only at the very end.'

'Did she threaten to tell your wife?'

'Yes. And I wouldn't have killed her even if she had.'

'Was she frightened of anyone?'

'No. She took karate lessons.'

'What about her ex-husband?'

Bowyer grinned. 'She used to take the mickey out of him. Impotence. She said that's what wrecked their marriage. And his conviction showed she'd been right.'

'Conviction?'

'He was caught with another man in a public lavatory. You must have it on file, surely?'

'Where were you on the night Barbara Sinclair was killed?'

'I was at home. My son was ill. The doctor came round.'

'That was at 8.45 p.m., sir. Where were you at 1 a.m.?'

'In bed, asleep.'

'And the night Dorothy Bowyer died?'

'The same, I expect. Earlier in the evening, my wife and I went to see a movie – *Terms of Endearment.*'

'Does your wife know about your affairs?'

'Probably.'

'What does that mean, exactly?'

'It means yes. That's how she won me – she was one of my affairs. I was very honest with her. She knew what I was like. I guess she still does.'

'How would you describe your relationship with her?'

'Pretty good. Very loving. We need each other. Ours is a solid marriage.'

'You're in a lot of trouble, Mr Bowyer. A lot of trouble.'

'I didn't do anything wrong.'

'Look at it from our point of view, sir. We have a suspect linked to two victims. We have a mask and a needle found at the suspect's home. And we have no alibis for the suspect on the nights of the murders. You could have slipped out of bed without your wife knowing.'

'Hardly likely.'

'Mrs Bowyer takes sleeping tablets, sir. Prescribed by Doctor Mitchell.'

'I didn't kill those women.'

Fletcher remembered the witness who saw a blue Sierra. A letter and a number matched Bowyer's plates. Keeping his voice low, his eyes locked to Bowyer's, he took a chance.

'But you were in Abbey Street the night Mary White was murdered.'

Bowyer's face fell. 'I know how this looks—'

'Just tell me about Abbey Street, sir.'

'I got a call from a man who said he knew about me and Barbara. He said he wanted a thousand pounds to keep quiet. I told him I only had two hundred. He said it would be a good down payment and I should be in Abbey Street at exactly 1.15 am. I was to wait twenty minutes while he checked if there were any police in the area.'

'And?' said Fletcher.

'He didn't show. Then I saw a police car pull up nearby and I drove home.'

Fletcher shook his head and grinned. 'You're in a mess, Jack. And you've lied to us – even if only by omission. You knew two of the victims and you were parked near the house of the fourth on the night she was murdered. What does that suggest to you?'

'I didn't do it.'

'But what *did* you do?'

'I don't understand,' said Bowyer.

Fletcher lit a cigarette and leaned back. 'I know you're

not the murderer, Mr Bowyer. What I need to know is, why are you in the frame?'

'You believe me? You actually believe me? Thank God!'

'It's nothing to do with God, sir, just police work. You see, the killer thinks we're a bunch of woodentops. He's gone to a lot of trouble to put you in the frame, but he's overlooked several points. Number one, Hilary Evans. Not exactly your biggest fan, is she? And yet she told us that the first Mrs Bowyer said she was being followed by a man in a blue car. You'd think your first wife would have recognised you. Secondly, the mask and needle. The killer would keep those where he keeps his combat trousers and trainers, not behind a piece of furniture in the living room. Also, the needle would have had sections of fingerprints on it. The killer – had it been you – wouldn't have cleaned the weapon quite so thoroughly, merely to leave it in a bag to be found. Thirdly, and most importantly, sir, is the semen found in two of the victims. It's now possible to establish the blood group of the assailant. His is group O. Yours is AB negative.'

'Then why am I here?'

'Because you must know the killer.'

'Why?'

'Because he hates you!' said Fletcher. 'Jesus, man, why do you think you've been set up?'

'I haven't the faintest idea.'

'Who has access to your house?'

'Access?'

'There's no sign of a break-in, so if you didn't put the mask and needle there, someone else must have done it. Who?'

'Who indeed?' said Bowyer. 'I'm not a popular man, I don't know why, but I haven't any enemies. Truly I haven't.'

'I was asking about access, sir?'

'Apart from my wife and children, I can't think of anyone. The insurance man? The window cleaner? Jehovah's Witnesses?'

'Well, you think about it, Mr Bowyer. Can I borrow your wedding ring?'

'Why?'

'Sentimental reasons,' snapped Fletcher. 'I am trying to help you, you know.'

Bowyer removed the ring, a plain gold band, and dropped it into Fletcher's outstretched palm.

Outside the room, Fletcher turned to Adams. 'I expect you to keep a lid on this. I don't want to read about Bowyer or the Deathmask in the morning papers.'

'Something's bound to get out, sir – the station's buzzing with it.'

'Just let it be known that the man who leaks the story will be wearing his balls as a necklace.'

'Are we any closer, sir? I mean, Bowyer damn near fitted the bill. No one else looks anywhere near likely for it.'

'Maybe. There's something nagging at the back of my mind, so I'll be going through the files again to keep worrying at it. I'll see you later.'

'What about Bowyer?'

'Get a car to take him home. Quietly!'

29

In a café in town, Mr Sutcliffe covered the scone with the last of the clotted cream and added a small mountain of strawberry jam to the top. It was early October.

'You're never going to eat all that!' said Ethel.

He grinned – and the scone disappeared. 'Had the British soldier been armed with scones and jam, your country would have conquered the world in half the time.'

'We don't like to do things quickly,' she said, smiling. 'And you have cream on your beard.'

'Thank you, Ethel.' He wiped it clean with a paper napkin and poured a second cup of tea from the stainless steel pot.

A waitress appeared. 'Will there be anything else?' she asked.

'Some more scones, please.'

'You *are* in good spirits today, Mr Sutcliffe,' said Ethel.

'I have always adored what you British call "window-shopping". I was raised in Matabeleland and was twelve before I saw the inside of a general store. I thought it a treasure house. When my father became rich and we travelled the world, I never ceased to marvel at the variety of luxuries for sale. I think perhaps there is truth in the old stories of missionaries and coloured beads. Once I thought I would sell my soul for a red silk shirt.'

'And did you?'

'No. My father bought one for me when I was at school in Switzerland.'

'That must have pleased you.'

'Some boys tore it from my back on my first day. I was never meant to have a red silk shirt.'

'I always wanted a sequinned coat, like the one Carole Lombard wore when she married Clark Gable. Padded shoulders and puff sleeves. It was sensational. I wanted blonde hair, too, just like hers.'

'Be honest, Ethel – you wanted to *be* Carole Lombard. You desired Gable.'

'We all did then. Or Cary Grant. And you?'

'I had no heroes of the screen. But I adored a young woman. Her name was Ayela. She became the mistress of a white farmer. Savage waste.'

'Is that why you never married?'

'Nothing so romantic. And I did marry, in 1947. She died of a fever four years later while I was fighting in Korea. There were no children.'

'Were you very much in love?'

He smiled. 'If I had been, I would not have reenlisted for another war in a land that was not mine.'

'Why did you do that?'

'I was planning ahead. I wanted to learn of military organisation and the use of weapons. I was determined to return to Matabeleland and drive the whites out of existence.'

'And now you are here with me. What changed you?'

'Nothing, Ethel. Were I twenty again, I would be in South Africa now. I got old.'

'That's not true. You're a gentle man – I don't see you as some bush terrorist.'

'You women are wondrous creatures. You bring out the best in a man, and it is all you see. All my life, I have been a hunter and a killer. A warrior, Ethel, from a long line of warriors. I have killed the lion and faced the terrors of the dark side.'

'But you always fought for what you felt was right.'

'No! To claim that would make me a hypocrite. There is no right. Rhodes took Matabeleland by conquest, with his machine guns. But the Matabele had taken it from the Mashona by conquest. It is an odd notion that right will prevail. It never has. You mentioned your own history once. Answer me this: if a man could prove he was the direct descendant of Harold of Hastings, would the Queen surrender her crown to him? All that counts is the status quo. But you British cannot understand that. It is why you have so much trouble in Ireland. You conquered it, and now you cannot hold it. But it is ours, you say. Nonsense. It belongs to whoever can take it. That is the lesson of history.'

'Then why did you fight?'

'Perhaps it was because I saw Ayela in bed with a white farmer. Perhaps it was because someone ripped my red silk shirt from my back. Who can tell? Perhaps I had a dream.'

The waitress arrived with more scones and Mr Sutcliffe devoured them at speed.

'I wish we'd not had that conversation,' said Ethel as they walked out into the sunshine. 'I feel quite low now.'

'I am sorry. But you see me through those rose-coloured spectacles.'

'You are wrong, Mr Sutcliffe, I see you as you are, but I choose to look at your best qualities. That is the real talent women have.'

His head came up and he swung around, eyes scanning the crowds milling in the shopping precinct.

'What is it?'

'Go home, Ethel. I will see you later.'

He moved off into the crowd, emptying his mind, focusing his talent. The emanation had been so strong that his soul had been catapulted to the bush. With three bullets in his back, he was already struggling to survive, and then he had felt the lion's presence, stalking him, moving silently through the undergrowth.

Here in West London, the same terrible sense of fear had descended like a sudden storm. Somewhere in this crowd, the beast was following his prey. Only this beast had a long needle and a black mask in place of claws and teeth.

His heart began to pound, and he calmed himself with steady, deep breathing.

Concentrate, Mangiwe. Seek the killer.

Ahead, into the supermarket. Mr Sutcliffe eased his way forwards, threading through the crowd.

'Oi! Watch who you're pushing!'

Mr Sutcliffe moved on.

'I'm talking to you, you black bastard.'

A large, pot-bellied man in a flat cap grabbed his arm. Mr Sutcliffe shook it loose and tried to walk away. A fist swung ponderously at his head. He blocked it with his forearm and sent the man spinning to the pavement with a left cross. Ignoring the furore around him, he ran several paces towards the supermarket, straining for the killer's spoor.

'Just a minute, sir!' said a young policeman.

'No time!' said Mr Sutcliffe.

The policeman stepped into his path. Mr Sutcliffe grabbed him by the jacket and hurled him onto the wire trolleys outside the main doors. He ran inside the supermarket, moving swiftly along the aisles.

Nothing.

Then he sensed the faintest trace from the far end of the store.

The car park exit!

He hurdled the barriers designed to keep trolleys inside the shop and loped up the incline, through the rubber swing doors – just in time to see a large blue car disappearing down the exit lane.

Behind him, two policemen were pounding up the slope. He turned and spread his hands.

'Be calm!' he said.

But the first flew at him, his face red with rage. Mr Sutcliffe hit him with a right cross that sent the man stumbling to his knees. The second man slowed and drew his truncheon.

'You asked for it,' he said.

'Do not be foolish,' warned Mr Sutcliffe. 'I desire none of this.'

''Course you don't,' said the officer. 'You bastard blacks think you can get away with anything. Well, not here, my lad.'

Mr Sutcliffe waited. The officer lunged, the truncheon whistling down. Mr Sutcliffe swayed back as the weapon flashed by his face then crashed a right uppercut to the officer's belly. The air whooshed from the man's lungs and his knees gave way. The first man was still struggling to regain his feet. Mr Sutcliffe ignored him and strolled from the car park.

If only he could have seen who the killer was following.

30

He fought to stay calm as the car pulled out into the busy street, his eyes flickering to the rear-view mirror, expecting at any moment to see the huge black man racing towards his car. But there was nothing. He drove east and parked in a quiet cul-de-sac.

Why had the man been chasing him? And what sixth sense had warned him to turn and see the giant figure bearing down, pushing his way through the crowd?

One fact was certain: the giant knew.

There was no doubt about that.

God, it was all going so wrong! Marry had been furious when Bowyer was freed, ranting and raging through the house. He'd done his best to bring calm but had been brushed aside. He knew why Marry felt such hatred for Bowyer. But they'd lost. And Marry couldn't see it.

And so they'd stopped for a few weeks, but now Marry said the killing had to go on.

He lit a cigarette and wound down the window. All the planning. All the clues. How could the police *not* accuse Bowyer? It was incomprehensible. Maybe they didn't know he'd been in Abbey Street, or had missed the connection between the similar number plates on the decoy blue Sierra and Bowyer's. Maybe they hadn't found out about his affair with the first whore. That had been Marry's reasoning, but he couldn't believe it.

All he knew was that the net was closing, and the dreams of the lion were worse than ever. When he was a boy, he used to have dreams that came true. He dreamed he saw Nigel from his class with a white face and grey eyes, and Nigel had died three weeks later. He'd never forget that. Never!

But what did the lion mean? There was no jungle in West London.

It means you're going to get caught, you fool, he told himself. He flicked the cigarette through the open window. It had to stop. He had to convince Marry.

He was in the clear at the moment. Nothing pointed to him. But who knew what errors lay ahead?

Marry would take some convincing. But then Marry was almost insane, he realised. The hatred of Bowyer was only an indication of a deeper turmoil, a childhood horror.

And nothing would erase the memory of the hanged man.

31

Stan King's trip to Buffalo, New York, had turned into a disaster. To begin with, we made a phone call to Dr Chan to check his progress every few days, and the answers weren't encouraging. Initial exploratory surgery had revealed little hope of even delaying the cancer's spread. Our calls became further and further apart. An air of gloom descended on the office, despite the fact he had survived longer than we had thought he could. Andrew Evans, our chief reporter, explained the newspaper's perspective.

'We shouldn't have sent him. It could screw up the next appeal.'

'I don't understand,' I said.

'It's simple, Jeremy. People like to respond to charity appeals, but only if they're successful. Otherwise they feel they've wasted their money. Next time around, they think twice.'

'I can't believe that.'

'It's true, lad, believe me. I worked in Swindon for several years and we had a beauty there. A little girl dying of leukaemia. A hospital in Florida claimed they could delay her death, so we launched an appeal and raised about four hundred quid. Not even enough for the fare. Then our editor, bless his cotton socks, came up with the answer. We carried a new story that said all the little girl really wanted was to see Disney World before she died. More than eight thousand pounds flowed in over the next eleven days. Get the picture?'

'You think we should fly Stan to Disney World?'

'No. I think we should start toning down the updates.'

The editor was back from his secondment to another title by then. I haven't mentioned him before, at least not by name. The reason is that I have no space for him in my memories. He was one of that new breed of newspaper editor – the manager. Show him a news item and he wanted to know if there was an advertising angle. Tell him there was a great story about a little old lady being ripped off by a discount superstore and he wanted to know if they advertised with us, and whether carrying the story would lose us their contract. In short, he was adored by the paper's owners for his commercial awareness and loathed by all of the editorial staff. His compliments were treated like poisoned chalices.

He didn't know he was loathed. He had a wonderful talent for self-deception. Or maybe he didn't care.

Why mention him now?

Because he betrayed a trust.

Everything had gone quiet at the office. There were no new leads on the murderer. I was on holiday at the time, spending a few days at home catching up on some writing. I was creating the perfect novel, a grim fantasy about a giant barbarian hacking his way through a savage world. Naturally he had muscles like hawser cables, women found him irresistible, and his enemies fell like wheat before a scythe.

Then the *Herald* came through the letter box. I couldn't believe the front-page lead. The banner headline was legible from the top of the stairs.

PSYCHIC IN HUNT FOR DEATHMASK

I snatched the paper from the mat. *Psychic Ethel Hurst is*

helping the police in their hunt for the murderer known as Deathmask…

Fifteen minutes later, I was in the editor's office. His name was Barry Hill. He was thirty-seven years old and best described by the word 'avuncular'.

'There's really no need to get so upset,' he told me. 'Sit down.' I did so, and lost the first round. He called out to his secretary, Thelma, and requested two coffees. 'Enjoying your holiday?'

'Stuff the holiday, Barry! I promised Ethel. And the police.'

'Listen to me, Jeremy – you have to take the global view. Sales always slip around now, but this year it's been a little worse than expected. We're four per cent down and the chairman is concerned. This story is just the tonic we need. We've boxed out another ten per cent and first reports say we're selling very well.'

'What has that got to do with anything? Read my lips – I made a promise.'

'In a perfect world, I would agree with you,' he said. 'But, sadly, this is not a perfect world. And the story may well help to catch the killer. All publicity should be welcomed.'

'And what about the danger to Ethel?'

'What danger? Let's not be melodramatic, Jeremy. He hasn't killed in ages, and he'd hardly be stupid enough—'

'To do another Mary White?'

'Exactly.'

'There used to be a time when integrity was part of this business.'

'And I regret its passing more than I can tell you,' he said. 'Now you head home and enjoy the rest of your holiday.'

I should have quit there and then but I didn't have the nerve. Not an easy thing to admit, especially when I'd spent the best part of three days writing about giant barbarian heroes.

I left his office and tried to find Don Bateman, but he was away for the rest of the week. That made me feel better. It would have been awful if Don had been part of this disgraceful episode.

As I left the building, I met Sue. We hadn't exchanged a word not related to work since our argument in Richmond Park. She looked beautiful in a simple white blouse, pink skirt and ankle boots.

'I'm sorry, Jem,' she said. 'It's disgusting.'

'That's newspapers.'

'No, that's Barry Hill. You fancy a drink?'

'Only if we don't talk about politics.'

'Agreed,' she said, linking her arm with mine. All the tension eased away. We sat in the lounge bar of the Barley Mow saying very little. She leaned close and kissed me.

Half an hour later, we were in bed at my flat and the world was a good place once more.

Sue returned to work, but came back that evening and we had a meal I'd spent the afternoon preparing. Pear halves stuffed with stilton and cream cheese, followed by Chicken Maryland. Sue was suitably complimentary; we left the washing up and adjourned to the lounge to finish the white wine.

'I heard a rumour today,' she said. 'The police had a suspect in custody but they let him go.'

'You're kidding? There's been nothing on the news.'

'They kept it secret, so I'm told.'

'Why the secrecy?' I said.

'Who knows? No comment from Morris or Beard, and I can't raise Fletcher.'

'That's incredible.'

'There's something else, too – there's a mask at the nick with the word DEATH embroidered on it.'

'You've got some good contacts.'

'Yes, I do. But no one's coming up with a name.'

'Have you told anyone?'

'I sold the tip to the *Mirror* for £200. Tomorrow's edition should be interesting.'

'Then it could be over? God, that would be great news.'

'I thought you'd be pleased. What's this?' she asked, picking up my manuscript.

'It's a novel I'm working on. Don't read it!' I took the manuscript from her and put it away in the bureau drawer.

'What kind of novel has a hero called Borak?'

'It's a fantasy.'

'Not one of those where the musclebound hero gets a hernia from all those kneeling women holding on to his thighs?'

'Good God no!'

'That's just as well,' she said, grinning. 'I've always felt there was something terribly sad about them.'

'Sad? In what way?'

'Well, the authors must have dreadful sexual hang-ups. Have you noticed how the heroes always have long swords which they keep plunging into their enemies? And then there's the giant worms and snakes and deep, dark caves. Makes me picture inoffensive little men with thick pebble glasses who have dominating wives or still live with their mothers.'

'Yes,' I agreed. 'Books like that are a joke.'

'I did a thesis on them at university. Do you know the Conan series?'

'I've heard of them,' I said, hoping she wouldn't look too

closely at my bookshelves, which contained every single volume.

'The author lived with his mum, and when she was dying, he shot himself. Sad, isn't it?'

'Very. More wine?'

'No thanks. I'd like to read your book. Let me take it with me.'

'No!' I replied, more sharply than I had intended. 'It's still a first draft.'

'Does the hero have a longsword?'

'No, he sets his enemies on fire using his thick pebble glasses. If that doesn't work, he sends his mother after them.'

She giggled. 'I've missed you, Jem. I never asked, did you get home all right from Richmond?'

'I walked.'

'I'm sorry.'

'Me, too.' She reached out and took my hand.

The doorbell rang.

I could have cried.

It was Ethel, and she was in a terrible state. I thought it would be about the paper, but I was wrong. 'It's the police,' she said. 'They've arrested Mr Sutcliffe.'

'Come in,' I told her, putting my arm round her shoulder. I helped her upstairs and tried to settle her in the lounge, but she wouldn't sit down. Her eyes were red and tearful. She didn't even appear to notice Sue sitting there.

'They came to his house and took him away. I tried to find out what they wanted him for, and they said he had hit a policeman. I don't know what to do.'

'I'll make you a cup of tea,' said Sue, rising.

'Oh, I'm sorry, Jeremy, you're entertaining.'

'Forget it. I'm glad you came. This is Sue Cater, a work-mate. Sue, Ethel Hurst.'

'Pleased to meet you,' said Sue.

'There's no tea. Make it a weak coffee.' I moved to the phone and rang the station. The desk sergeant was some-one I knew, Frank Anderson. Nice man, but with breath that spoke of chemical warfare. I could almost smell it down the phone.

'Sutcliffe?' he said. 'The big black bugger? Yes, he's here. Coming up before the bench tomorrow morning.'

'Any chance of him being released tonight?'

'None whatsoever, Jeremy. He broke PC Simpson's ribs.'

'Is he all right?'

'Yes, he's all strapped up now.'

'No, I meant Sutcliffe.'

'Why shouldn't he be?'

'Nothing to do with you, but although he doesn't look it, he's sixty-nine years old and he's got a serious heart con-dition.'

'Straight up? No bullshit?'

'Gospel, Frank.'

'Okay,' he said and rang off. The speed of his departure worried me.

'Is he all right?' asked Ethel.

'Yes. He's coming up at the magistrates' court tomorrow. Why did he do it?'

'I don't know. He was in a strange mood, but he didn't tell me that anything had happened. They won't send him to prison, will they?'

'I don't know, Ethel. I'm sorry. Depends who's on the bench. If it's Jardine, they probably will. He doesn't like blacks. I'll talk to Ray Morris in the morning.'

I drove Ethel home, then Sue.

The following morning, I spoke to Morris, but he wasn't happy with the thought of leniency for Mr Sutcliffe.

'You have to understand, Jeremy, that given how things are in Lansdowne, we can't have a man getting away with assaulting two police officers. I'm surprised there wasn't another riot when we took him in; they seem to happen every week.'

'That's because he's not popular there. He's against violence.'

'Looks like it. Robinson lost two teeth and Simpson's got busted ribs.'

'I can't think why he'd do it.'

'I don't much care why, son. He did it, and now he's got to pay for it.'

'Did he say anything when he was arrested?'

'Nothing. Not a word. Still hasn't.'

'Can I talk to him?'

'For what purpose?'

'I don't know, Superintendent, but can I?'

'You'd better be quick. He's up before Jardine in an hour.'

I saw Mr Sutcliffe in his cell. His face was grim and set, just like the first time I encountered him. He was sitting on the narrow cot bed. He'd been relieved of his shoelaces and his belt.

'Ethel's very worried,' I said as the steel door closed behind me.

He nodded. 'You broke your promise to her. You published her name.'

'I was on holiday. I didn't know they were doing it.'

'Maybe not. But it was your promise.'

'I know it was wrong. But I'm here to help you. If I can.'

'What can you do?'

'I can speak for you in court. Tell me why you did it.'

'I was hunting a lion, Jeremy. And they tried to stop me.'

'I don't understand.'

'It is not important. I was foolish. How are the policemen?'

'They'll live.'

'Yes. I am not as strong as once I was. I almost had him, Jeremy. The killer. He was following another victim. You must find her.'

'How? Did you see her?'

'No. But she was shopping in Tesco's, or else she passed through there to the car park.'

'I see. I'll check it out. Now, what about you? Will you tell the magistrates you were hunting a lion?'

'I shall say nothing.'

'They could put you in prison.'

'It does not matter.'

'It does to Ethel. Don't be so bloody selfish!'

He smiled then. 'What would you have me say?'

'Say someone picked your pocket and you were chasing them. When the policemen arrived, you were distraught. Something like that.'

'I do not wish to lie. They attacked me, Jeremy. With truncheons.'

'Surprise, surprise. Facing a black giant with shoulders like a truck, what would you do?'

He smiled at that.

As usual, there were three magistrates on the bench, but the one who counted was Lieutenant Colonel Wilbur Jardine, a cool ex-professional soldier with views to the right of mine. As far as he was concerned, Attila the Hun was a wet leftie.

I sat on the press bench with Phil Deedes, who was covering the case.

Mr Sutcliffe had spurned representation.

He was asked how he pleaded to the charge of assaulting PC Albert Robinson, causing actual bodily harm.

'Guilty,' he said.

'And to the charge of assaulting PC Kenneth Simpson and causing him actual bodily harm?'

'Guilty.'

'Very well. Normally I would let the witnesses stand down, but I wish to have some explanation for your behaviour. We will proceed.'

The first witness for the prosecution was PC Albert Robinson. He was sworn in and produced his notebook. Prosecuting counsel was Victor Burgess, a tall, skeletal figure more suited to undertaking. He stood and began his cross-examination.

'Could you outline the events of yesterday, Constable Robinson?'

'Yes, sir. I was on foot patrol in the precinct when I observed the defendant strike a member of the public. I approached him and began to speak with him. He took me by the jacket and threw me to the ground. He ran into the Tesco store and I pursued him. I was joined by PC Simpson, who had observed the incident from his patrol vehicle. We caught the defendant in the car park and requested him to come quietly, whereupon he attacked us both. I was struck on the jaw. PC Simpson received a blow to his ribs, which cracked two of them.'

'And what injuries did you sustain, Officer?'

'Two teeth were cracked and had to be removed, sir.'

Jardine leaned forward. 'Did he appear to you to be on drugs, Officer?'

'I couldn't say, Your Worship.'

'Go on, Officer,' said Burgess.

'Myself and three other officers made extensive inquiries

and ascertained that the defendant's description matched that of a Mr Mangiwe Sutcliffe. We went to his house and arrested him.'

'Was there any further violence?'

'None, sir.'

'Thank you, Officer.' Burgess sat down.

'Well, Mr Sutcliffe,' said Jardine, leaning forward again, 'do you have any questions for the officer?'

'None, sir.'

'Were the events as outlined accurate?'

'Indeed they were.'

'Mr Burgess – do you wish to add further to your case?'

'Yes, Your Worship,' he said, rising. 'The defendant is a sixty-nine-year-old Rhodesian who took up British nationality at the end of the unrest. He is a former soldier in the British Army who served with the Eighth Army in Egypt during the Second World War. He was awarded the Military Medal and was twice mentioned in despatches. He also fought in Korea. Nothing is known about the defendant in terms of any criminal background.'

'Do you have anything to say?' said Jardine, flicking a finger in Mr Sutcliffe's direction.

'What would you have me say, sir?'

'You could begin by giving a reason for your attack.'

Mr Sutcliffe shrugged. 'I can think of nothing that would satisfy you. I lost my temper and now I must pay for it. I do not complain.'

'Do you have any regrets?'

'Of course. I am sorry the officers were hurt, and I am thankful the injuries were not more serious.'

Jardine conferred quietly with his two colleagues then leaned forward.

'On the first charge, you will receive three months in

prison, and on the second charge, three months in prison, the sentences to run consecutively, making a term of six months in all.' He paused. 'This sentence will be suspended for two years. Do you understand what that means?'

'No, Your Worship.'

'It means it will hang over you. If you break the law again within that two-year period, it will be brought into effect immediately. We have taken this lenient course because you pleaded guilty and were ready to accept responsibility for your actions. This court has heard too many whinging, whining defendants, blaming the police, society or God Almighty for their own shortcomings. Step down!'

Phil Deedes tapped me on the shoulder. 'Your man's bloody lucky.'

'It's a miracle,' I said.

'Not at all. Jardine served with the Eighth Army. And the old pal's act overcomes anything – including racial bigotry.'

I was looking forward to telling Ethel, who hadn't been able to bring herself to attend. Sutcliffe had been lucky.

32

Mark Fletcher was furious as he sat in Ethel's small front room, a copy of the *Daily Mirror* in his lap. DEATHMASK: MAN ARRESTED AND FREED screamed the headline. Beneath it was a photograph of Jack Bowyer.

'Is he the man, Inspector?' asked Ethel.

'You tell me, Mrs Hurst,' answered Fletcher, offering Ethel the thick gold wedding band.

She hesitated, rubbing her hands together as if cold. Slowly she reached out, her fingers closing around the metal as Fletcher dropped it into her palm. She relaxed almost at once. Then she smiled.

'He really is a bit of a ram, isn't he? He reminds me of my late husband, Freddie.'

'But is he the killer?'

'No. He's a deeply sad man frantically searching for the secret of happiness. He won't find it.'

'You're sure he's not the murderer?'

'As sure as you are, Mr Fletcher. There is something of you in this ring.'

Fletcher smiled thinly, uncomfortable now. Leaning forward, he lifted his cup and sipped the hot tea. 'Do you mind if I smoke?'

'Please do. Mr Sutcliffe is very angry at the *Herald* for printing my name. Do you think I am in any danger?'

'I don't think so. Most people regard psychics as a bit of a joke.'

'I'm not sure that's reassuring,' she told him.

He lit a cigarette and gratefully inhaled.

'Will you let the man go?'

'I already did – well before I saw this newspaper article. He was set up, Mrs Hurst, and in doing that, the killer made his first real mistake. I should have him soon.'

'I hope you are right. Mr Sutcliffe almost caught him the other day.'

'What?'

'My friend Mr Sutcliffe – he picked up the killer's aura in the supermarket. He was following another victim.'

'He "picked up his aura"?'

'Yes.'

Fletcher shook his head. 'Did he have a long black cape and fangs?'

'You shouldn't mock, Mr Fletcher.'

'It's hard not to, Mrs Hurst. Is your friend looking for some publicity?'

'I rather think not. You should speak to him.'

'Another time. Just tell him to keep a wooden stake handy. Thanks for the tea.'

Outside, a gang of youths were congregating around Fletcher's car. He moved through them, sensing the tension.

'Bastard pig,' said one of them as he opened the driver's door. Fletcher ignored the comment, gunned the engine and pulled away.

Back at the station, John Adams brought him a cup of black coffee and the two men compared notes.

'There was no sign of a break-in at the Bowyer house,' Adams began. 'Mrs Bowyer claims she's had no visitors for a week, and she moved that wall unit only two days ago.'

'What are the locks like?' asked Fletcher.

'They've a double-locked double-glazed patio door and safety chains on front and back. All the windows have secondary double glazing and Mrs Bowyer checks they're closed every evening.'

'Still not impossible to break in without leaving a trace. Just unlikely,' said Fletcher. 'So, it's fair to assume that whoever left the items either had a key or was a welcome visitor.'

'I'd say so,' agreed Adams.

'Get a list of all friends and nearby relatives. Do they have a cleaning woman?'

'I didn't ask. Sorry.'

'Do it now.'

After Adams had gone, Fletcher returned to his files. The clues were there, but he couldn't see them. That was what always irritated him about murder inquiries. Plain as the nose on your face – but only in hindsight. And the newspapers were so good at hindsight. He opened the file on Gary Sinclair, now brought up to date with the conviction for gross indecency in May 1986. Computer error had been blamed for its omission. According to the evidence, Sinclair had waited for almost an hour in a public convenience in Shepherds Bush before approaching a young black man. They were spotted by two officers stationed on the roof.

Bloody waste of time, thought Fletcher. Who cared if two consenting adults wanted to play with each other in a poxy bog?

He thought of that poor sodding actor whose career had been ruined by just such a conviction. Rape figures up, muggings on the increase, burglaries soaring, and here were two constables lying on a toilet roof, desperate to catch a couple of fairies.

He closed the file and lit a cigarette.

His coffee was now cold, but he drank it anyway.

Bowyer was innocent but still the key, somehow. The killer had tried to frame Bowyer, and with a fraction more effort might have succeeded. Why?

'Why?' he said, aloud.

'The eternal question,' said Ray Morris.

Fletcher stood hastily. 'Sorry, sir, didn't see you come in.'

'Sit down, Mark. How are things progressing?'

'Almost there, sir. I can feel it.'

'But not Bowyer?'

'No, sir. I even took his ring to Mrs Hurst. She confirmed it.'

'Shame.'

'Yes. We've missed something.'

'Any ideas?'

'Not at the minute.'

'Keep on it, Mark. You'll crack it. By the way, you heard about Seymour?'

'Seymour Holding?'

'Yes. Busted out of the Scrubs last night.'

Fletcher swore. 'The man's a total nutter.'

'And he'll be back on Lansdowne by now. It won't be much fun pulling him in.'

'He'll be at his sister's.'

'That's my guess. You got time to handle it?'

'Yes, but we'll need to go in mob-handed. And there could be a flare-up.'

'Get in and out as fast as you can.'

'Four cars and the van ought to do it. Twenty officers.'

'I'll leave it to you.'

'He's a gun-freak, sir. We'll have to go in armed.'

'You and Adams are cleared for firearms duty. Check your weapons out.'

Within the hour, Fletcher was standing at the board in the briefing room, studying the faces of the twenty officers who would be joining him on the raid.

'This has got to be quick,' he said. 'No longer than fifteen minutes, arrival to departure. Sergeant Adams and myself will be armed. Seymour Holding, as most of you know, was serving eight years for double rape. He's also known to be a gun collector, handguns. When he was arrested last year, we found two Colt Pythons, a Smith and Wesson .357, and a Colt Commander .45 hidden in his flat. There could have been others elsewhere, so be careful. But even without a gun he's a big bugger. If he runs, tackle him hard. You've all seen the mug shots. You know who we're looking for. Stay alert.'

'What sort of backup have we got?' asked a young constable.

'You think maybe the army should stand by, son?'

'No, sir. But Lansdowne's on the edge of a riot as it is.'

'I know. In and out fast is the best option we have. But all other divisions are on call in case there's an explosion.'

'That still makes it two hours before riot control get there,' put in another officer.

'Then let's make sure there's no riot,' said Fletcher.

33

Rain pounded at the window and lightning speared the sky in the distance. I switched off the overhead light and sat by the window, watching the storm roll across London. Sue was stretched out on the sofa reading a magazine by the light of the standard lamp, Rascal curled on her lap.

It was a fine night to be indoors.

'I saw Martin Dunn today,' said Sue. 'He asked to be remembered to you.'

I turned back. 'How is he?'

'Bronzed and fit. He's been on a business trip to Miami. He brought me back a pair of cowboy boots. They're terrific.'

'I've always wanted a John Wayne hat,' I told her.

'I might have guessed he'd be a hero of yours.' She held up her hands. 'I'm sorry. Pax. It just slipped out. Anyway, maybe he bought you one.'

'Did you tell him how Stan's getting on in the States?'

Sue pushed Rascal from her lap and sat up. 'Yes,' she said, sadly. 'He was pretty upset.'

'Martin's a nice guy. How did you meet?'

'I was doing an advertising feature on his business and he took me to lunch.'

'Did he make a pass?' I asked, reddening.

'Of course he didn't. And I thought you weren't going to ask about my previous boyfriends?'

'I know. But you weren't going to mention politics, either.'

'Touché,' she said, grinning. 'You really are quite naïve, though, for a fascist.'

'How do you work that out?'

'Well, you're the only man I've met who didn't realise in an instant that Martin was gay.'

'Gay? He never made a pass at me!'

Sue shrieked with delight. 'How quaint!' she mocked. 'He can't be gay because he didn't try to sleep with gorgeous Jem.'

'That's not what I meant,' I snapped. Then I grinned. 'Well, maybe it is. But how can people tell? I mean, he doesn't wear lipstick or anything.'

'Oh, Jem, you're perfect. Promise me you'll never change.'

I made the promise, hand on heart. Sue stretched. She was still a little stiff and suffered occasional headaches. But apart from that and a thin scar on her forehead, no one would ever guess she'd been an inch from death in a serious car crash not so long ago.

'Did he tell you he was gay?' I asked, following her into the kitchen, where she filled her glass with the rest of the white wine I'd bought that evening.

'No, of course not.'

'Then how can you be sure?'

'I'll tell you when you're older. Anyway, what difference does it make? He's still a nice man.'

'It must hurt his parents,' I said.

'No idea,' said Sue. 'As far as I recall from the piece I did on him, his parents are dead. Bit of a sad story, really. You know Don Dodds, the SOCO at the nick? He told me Martin's father killed himself. And Martin found the body.'

'God, that must have been terrible. I'm amazed he turned out as well as he did.'

'What does that mean? It's not a mental illness, you know,' said Sue, turning on me.

'Oh yes, sorry. For a moment there, I forgot you were a leftie. No, excuse me, there's absolutely nothing wrong with being a fairy. Every home should have one.'

Her face went white and her eyes flashed. 'You really are an idiot sometimes, Jem. A grade-one pillock!'

I had sense enough to realise this time that if she left now she'd never be back. 'I'm sorry,' I said. And I meant it. 'Maybe I was born out of my time.'

'Yeah,' she agreed. 'You'd have been a big hit in Nazi Germany.'

'Blimey, Martin's not Jewish as well, is he?'

Timing is everything. She took one look at my face and burst into laughter. 'You prat!' she said. I nodded.

'I'm really not that bad. I've seen *The Naked Civil Servant* three times, and I even saw Quentin Crisp's one-man show. Honest. Cross my heart and hope to die in a cellar full of pansies.'

She forgave me.

When Don Bateman returned from his break, he had a furious row with Barry Hill over the Ethel story. We all heard it reverberating through the walls. Don ought to have been fired for some of the names he called the editor, but then everyone knew Hill was weak. He'd sit there wearing an inane grin, his nostrils flaring out like snail shells, and allow the storm to wash over him.

I was delighted to hear Bateman powering in. I wish I'd had the nerve to do it.

'It doesn't mean anything,' said Andrew Evans, flicking on the kettle and preparing coffee for the reporters. 'Don'll shout and make himself feel better, but nothing will get done. In some ways, they're as bad as each other.'

'That's unfair,' put in Sue. 'At least Don cares about the reporters – and about editorial integrity.'

'Maybe,' said Andrew. 'But he'll shout at Barry and then let it drop. He won't sound off to the chairman. He knows he wouldn't get away with it.'

I didn't want to believe it, but I guess it was true. Later, when the row was over, Don sent Sue and me to interview Jack Bowyer, but he was taking no callers.

I'd spent some time interviewing staff at Tesco's, trying to identify the woman Mr Sutcliffe had said was shopping there, but had no luck. As a last move, I tried to locate Martin Dunn, to see if his computer magic could come up with any more details on the women from the marriage spread, even taking the other names my colleagues had already tried to trace. But even there I was thwarted. His secretary told me he'd taken the day off to see a friend. On the off chance that he might be at home, I drove to the east end of town to the large detached property he owned there. There were three cars in the drive, one of which was Martin's grey Jag.

Ringing the doorbell brought no response so I wandered around to the back of the house, calling as I came. There was a covered swimming pool behind the house. I slid open the double-glazed door and stepped inside. Martin was lying on a sunbed beside the pool. He switched off the ultraviolet tubes and rolled to his feet.

'Hello, Jem. Fancy a cold beer?'

'Are you kidding? It's nearly winter.'

'Not in here. The temperature and humidity of the Bahamas. Isn't it amazing what money can buy?'

I felt ill at ease. A cushioned sunlounger still showed the indentation of a body, and a second glass sat beside Martin's on the round white patio table. It wouldn't have bothered me if Sue hadn't told me he was gay. 'Am I interrupting something?' I said, pointing at the second glass.

'You're not interrupting anything,' he replied, noting my concern. 'I had a guest, but he's gone. Sit down and take your jacket off.'

I did so and he poured me a cold Budweiser.

'What can I do for you?'

I outlined my various problems and he grinned. 'So this giant witch doctor thought he saw the killer in Tesco's? Good God, Jeremy, isn't this a bit sensational for the poor old *Herald*? *News of the World*, maybe.'

I grinned, somewhat self-consciously. 'I know it sounds weird, but I honestly believe he's gifted.'

'Like the old lady who's psychic and helping the police?'

'Exactly.'

'Oh, come on! Hunting killers with tea leaves? It's a joke, Jem. The police are making themselves laughing stocks.'

'You haven't met Ethel, Martin. She's fantastic. She's re-lived all the murders and given the police tremendous help. All she needs is a piece of metal which the victim had near their skin and she can picture the moment of death. It's amazing. You know that policeman who was killed? Well, Ethel was inside his mind, and when she experienced the moment of his death, her eye went completely bloodshot. She's genuine. As soon as the killer leaves anything behind, she'll have him.'

'Well, she's obviously taken you in, dear boy. Another beer?'

'No thanks. Lovely garden. Not often you see roses still in bloom this time of the year.'

'I adore them. They're pretty sheltered back here, plus there's the spill-off heat from the pool. I think I have almost every variety there is.'

'Aren't they a little close together?' I asked, pointing to the nearest bed, where a yellow rose with pink-edged leaves was winding through a thick growth of reddish blooms.

'I'll have to sack the gardener,' he said. 'So what did you want me to do?'

'Check if there are any possible victims we may have missed. I thought maybe we could look into the women who moved away.'

'For the witch doctor?'

'He's not a witch doctor! He's psychic. He says there's another killing planned.'

'What a weird world we're living in, to be sure,' said Martin, slipping on a pair of sunglasses and lying back on the sunbed. 'Can it wait until tomorrow?'

'Sure. I'm sorry to bother you with it.'

'It's no bother, Jem. How's Sue now? She wouldn't let on to me how she actually felt.'

'Still gets a little stiff, but she's mostly over the crash.'

'I'm glad. Give her my regards.'

'I will,' I said, rising. 'I'd best be getting back.'

'Stay for a swim,' he offered. 'I have a spare costume you can use.'

'I'm trying to turn over a new leaf and work for a change. Thanks anyway.'

Back at the office, I finished off a short story about roadworks causing havoc in Belnay Road and started a second about the local MP's trip to Romania.

Then, as they say in every bad movie, all hell broke loose.

34

He stepped from the sanctuary of the house to the pool where Marry was lying on the sunbed.

'You heard?' asked Marry, his body bathed in ultraviolet light.

'I heard. What are we going to do?'

Marry flicked off the tubes and sat, removing the polarised glasses. 'What choice do we have? These "psychics" will have to go. Jeremy, too.'

'That's insane, Marry. I can't! I thought we were going to stop.'

'Think about it, lover. I left the needle at Bowyer's. I used it on your wife. If they take that to this ... this witch woman, maybe she'll identify me. I doubt I held it long enough for her powers to work, if Jeremy is right, but I can't take the risk.'

Gary Sinclair sank back into the lounge chair and drained his whiskey. Where had it all gone wrong? It had started so perfectly. After meeting Martin, they'd enjoyed a whirlwind romance, and the handsome young computer genius had taken him on a fabulous trip across Europe. It had been the happiest time of Gary's life.

Then the bitch started her affair with Bowyer. He saw her outside Tesco's late one night and watched as Bowyer fondled her. She spotted him and walked over. Before he could stop himself, he said, 'Still acting the whore, Barbara?'

He should have known better. He'd never been able to beat her.

'Acting the whore?' mocked Barbara. 'At least I don't do it in public lavatories with black men.' My God! There were a dozen people close by, and Bowyer had grinned at him. Gary had turned and run.

Martin was furious when he told him. 'Should have killed the bitch,' he said. 'They're all the same.'

Gary had never seen Martin so upset. But he hadn't known then about Martin's father, who killed himself a year after his promiscuous wife left him for another man. Martin and his sister had been brought up by foster parents, and Marry had never recovered from the emotional shock of finding his father hanging from the banister rail.

Then the Amsterdam trip came up and Martin offered to kill Barbara while he was away. At first, Gary was horrified, but gradually he found the prospect more and more inviting. The plan was simple. Martin would murder Barbara, and Gary, on his return, would execute Bowyer's first wife. The police would suspect Bowyer because of his association with both women.

Only the woodentops hadn't made the connection.

Then Martin, with his magic computers, had come up with another plan while looking at the old copy of the *Herald* containing the 4-page wedding special. Find and butcher other whores who were married at the same time as Bowyer. Force the police to arrest him. Make him look like a crazy psychopath! But it had all gone wrong when that journalist had intervened, and then they'd had to kill the boyfriend, and then the policeman …

'Penny for your thoughts, lover?' asked Marry.

Gary looked into Martin's eyes and saw the madness lurking there.

'We'll never get away with it.'

'Why not? The old witch is sixty-four and lives alone. And Jeremy says Sutcliffe is almost seventy with a weak heart.'

'It's gone too far, Marry. Way too far.'

'Yes. It has. But you know something? I've enjoyed every minute of it. We'll take out the pair of them tonight. And then I'll pay Jeremy a visit.'

'Why him? He doesn't know anything.'

'He's not a fool, lover. When the old dear dies he'll put two and two together.'

Gary stood and walked to the pool, looking down at the water rippling around the whirl-jets. 'It's never going to stop, is it? We'll just keep on killing and killing, won't we?'

'Whatever you say, lover.'

Four police cars and a large black van screamed into the concrete yard of Beverley Towers. Fourteen officers scrambled clear and raced for the two stairwells at either end of the block. Six men remained with the vehicles.

Fletcher took the lead at the right stairwell, his snub-nosed Smith and Wesson still holstered at his belt. He powered his way up to the fourth floor two steps at a time, outdistancing the panting officers behind him. On the third floor, he passed a young boy sitting on the stairs, a syringe in his hand. He hurdled the stunned youth and moved up to the next landing, pleased to arrive before the younger Adams. Several seconds later, he saw the burly sergeant step onto the landing, his weapon in hand. Furious, he gestured for Adams to put away the gun. Adams did so, looking shame-faced.

Taking a deep breath, Fletcher walked along the landing, looking for flat 117. He tapped on the frosted glass. There was no reply.

'She gone out,' said a woman from the next flat. 'Ain' nobody home.'

'Kick it in,' said Fletcher, stepping aside and allowing a uniformed officer to move forward.

As the man prepared to smash the door down, there was a loud report from within the flat and the frosted glass exploded outwards. The policeman pitched backwards, toppling over the parapet. Fletcher leapt and grabbed the man's tunic. The dead weight hauled the inspector over the edge. Instinctively, his left arm hooked over the parapet, the stone cutting into his forearm. The constable was unconscious, blood staining the front of his uniform and flowing up over his collar, red droplets flying in the wind to spatter the ground some sixty feet below. Fletcher fought down the rising tide of panic as he felt himself slowly being torn from his hold. To survive, he knew he'd have to drop the wounded man to his death, but he couldn't bring himself to do it. Another shot sounded from behind him, and another. Then several pairs of hands grabbed him, hauling him to safety and carefully lifting the injured man onto the landing.

Fletcher's heart was pounding. He turned and saw the front door of flat 117 smashed from its hinges. Adams was standing in the hallway. Fletcher moved in alongside him – and saw the bodies.

Seymour Holding was lying face upwards on the thick white carpet, dead eyes staring sightlessly at the ceiling, his white shirt covered in blood. Beside him was a child of around seven. A bullet had torn half his face away. There was no sign of the sister.

Fletcher ordered his men down to the van, to get the injured officer out and fast. He gestured for four of them to stay with him.'I didn't see him,' whispered Adams, white-faced.

'Walker smashed the door in and there was another shot. I returned fire.'

Fletcher knelt beside Holding. There was a small entrance wound in his chest; the exit wound was a bloody hole in the man's side. 'How many shots did you fire?'

Adams flicked open the chamber. 'One, sir.'

'The boy was standing beside him. Your shot must have ricocheted from Holding's spine, come out between the ribs and then hit the boy. Fuck it!'

'Things are getting ugly outside, sir,' said an officer.

'Well, going in and out fast isn't an option now,' said Fletcher. 'Radio for backup.'

A woman's scream came from the hallway. It was the next-door neighbour, a fat woman in a multicoloured print dress.

'They've murdered him!' she shouted from the balcony. 'They've murdered the baby!'

'Get her inside her flat!' shouted Fletcher.

But it was too late. Scores of people had already gathered in the concrete square below and more lined the other landings. A brick sailed down, bouncing from the roof of one of the police cars. Bottles and stones hurtled after it. Fletcher ran onto the landing. Below, four men were trying to carry the injured officer to the van. One went down, then another.

'Get the van to them!' shouted Fletcher.

The black van slewed across the courtyard, its windscreen smashed. The injured men were helped inside, then all of the cars hurtled from sight.

'You're dead, man!' yelled someone from the opposite landing. Fletcher swung around. He had four uniformed officers and Adams. 'You hear me, man? Dead. We'll have your pigging head on a pole!'

'Adams!'

'Sir?'

'Things are going to get a little rough.'

'Yeah. I can almost hear the drums.'

'You will later, son. Walker, Pierce – stay on the landing and give a shout if anyone starts gathering on the stairwells,' ordered Adams. The two men started moving. Both were grim-faced.

'Bastard bad luck about the boy,' said Fletcher, pulling his cigarettes from his pocket. 'Oh, sod it!'

'What's wrong, sir?'

'I've only got three left. Should have stopped on the way.'

'You think they'll attack us?'

'Count on it.'

'We've got the firearms, sir.'

'With only a handful of rounds between us, and maybe a few more of Seymour's. You ever heard of the classic no-win situation, Adams? Well, this is it. Use the guns and we'll be pilloried for panicking. Without them, we'll probably be dead. Nice, eh?'

'It may not come to that, sir. It could all die down.'

A muffled explosion sounded from the street beyond the towers, followed by the sound of distant cheering.

'What the hell was that?' said Adams.

'That was a car's petrol tank exploding. I hope you didn't make too many plans for this evening.'

'Nothing that won't keep. You?'

'They're coming, sir!' shouted PC Walker, moving back along the landing. It pleased Fletcher that the officer didn't run. He patted the man's shoulder.

'This way, too, sir!' called PC Pierce, moving back to join the CID men.

'Watch the right, John,' said Fletcher, opening his coat and unclipping the retainer from his hip holster.

'Looks like they've brought in the local boss man,' whispered Walker.

'Good afternoon, Mr Gibson,' said Fletcher, moving forward.

'I demand to see the inside of Miss Holding's home,' said Jeremiah Gibson.

'I am afraid you'll have to wait, sir, until the scene investigators have finished.'

'Kill the pig!' shouted someone from the back. The crowd pushed forward. Gibson threw out his arms and the movement subsided.

'Is it true you have killed a child?'

'I'm afraid a child did die as a result of the shooting, Mr Gibson, but you can rest assured, my officer did not fire first.'

'You come into Lansdowne like cowboys blasting your guns at anything that moves!' yelled Gibson. 'And then you expect us to sit back and do nothing while you doctor the evidence.'

'That's not true, sir, and you're only inflaming the situation. Why don't you advise these people to go home?'

'Because they are here for justice. And they will have it!'

'Do you normally look for justice carrying pickaxe handles and knives? And is that a machete I see?'

'This is your last opportunity to step aside,' said Gibson.

'No, sir. This is *your* last opportunity to clear the landing,' said Fletcher, 'otherwise I shall arrest you for inciting a breach of the peace.'

Gibson laughed in his face. The crowd surged once more. Fletcher's gun rammed up under Gibson's chin, cocked and ready, against all of his training.

'Back off!' bellowed Fletcher. 'Now!' He could sense Pierce raising his gun as well.

'By God, you'll pay for this outrage,' hissed Gibson. 'Every one of you murderers will pay.'

Fletcher leaned in close. 'But not right this minute, eh, Mr Gibson, sir?'

Holding the gun under Gibson's chin, the detective inspector pushed him back into the mob. Slowly the crowd made space, moving towards the left-hand stairwell. Adams and Walker forced the crowd on the right side of the flat to retreat.

Once at the stairwell, Fletcher released the community leader.

'Now let's have a little bit of calm, shall we? I don't want to see anyone on this landing. You understand that, Mr Gibson?'

Gibson turned without answering and pushed his way through the crowd. Fletcher met the eyes of the remaining men.

'Return to your homes, gentlemen, please,' said Fletcher. 'You're probably missing a good evening on the telly.'

'We'll be back,' said one man. 'And don't think we can't match that,' he said, pointing to the gun.

Fletcher said nothing.

It was going to be a long night.

35

Out in the Atlantic, a standard wave depression began to deepen into a minor gale heading for the Bay of Biscay. There was nothing unusual about this, and minor gale warnings were issued by European weather stations. Fuelled by blustery winds, the storm struck a barrier of warmer air, bringing increased temperatures to one flank. The wind speed picked up. Thirty knots. Forty.

And the storm gathered momentum, turning sharply northwards from Biscay towards the coast of Devon. The depression deepened and deepened, and the gale grew from an angry child to a ravening beast, chasing its own tail, driving itself faster and faster. Wind speeds soared. Fifty knots. Sixty.

It struck the coast of Britain like the hammer of God, uprooting trees whose roots were already saturated by three weeks of rain, ripping down fences, tearing at roofs.

Seventy knots. The storm savaged the south. A cargo ship caught the brunt of its rage and was driven onto the beach near Dover.

In Hastings, the largest hotel quivered and a huge chimney stack smashed through the roof, killing a man in his bed and burying his wife alive. Another man was crushed by a fishing hut.

The monster sped on, winds close to 100 miles per hour clawing millions of trees from the ground, blocking roads, crushing cars. Gables collapsed, windows exploded, roofs were rendered to matchwood.

Like some vast mythical beast, the newborn hurricane roared towards London.

I was sitting chatting to Phil Deedes and Sue when Andrew Evans came in with news of the Lansdowne riot. Some four hundred policemen were on their way with full riot gear and a mounted section had been drafted in from Hammersmith. The picture Andrew painted was dreadful: cars overturned and torched, makeshift barricades and burning buildings. And six policemen were reported trapped at the centre of the estate in Beverley Towers.

Our photographer and three freelances were already in the area, and Sue and Phil were ordered out to join them. Don Bateman telephoned our production centre with a request for a late story to be allowed. This never went down well with the composing room. If our paper was late, other publications due to go to press after the *Herald* would be delayed, creating a backlog on the press. These delays would filter down to the external commercial contracts, causing loss of business and revenue.

'There's a bastard riot, for God's sake!' Bateman screamed down the phone. 'You want us to ignore it?'

This, apparently, got through to the man. Bateman spoke to him for about thirty seconds then put down the receiver. 'We have an extra two hours. Let's hope the police can establish control by then.'

'I can't see it, Don,' I said.

John French agreed. He took off his thick, black-framed glasses and rubbed his eyes.

'Listen, mate,' he said, 'we have two options – go with what we know, or write a chancer.'

'I hate chancers,' said Bateman. 'Let's see what happens.'

I knew what he meant. The *Herald* would be on the streets tomorrow come what may, and every reader would expect full coverage of the riot. But our story would have to be completed by 9 p.m. We could take a chance and write that police quelled the riot, making it sound as if we were up to the minute, but if the riot continued after that and there were deaths or other dramas after we went to press, our story would look ridiculous.

Nine months before, in the depths of winter, we'd been left with egg on our faces when an elderly man went missing, only to be found suffering with frostbite on a piece of waste ground behind the supermarket. At the last minute, we stripped in a front-page lead under the banner headline THE SURVIVOR. The man died twenty minutes after our deadline, and the morning radio news made our lead sound grossly inappropriate.

'We're not a newspaper any more,' hissed Don. 'We're a bastard advertising sheet. I don't know why I stick it.'

'Let's plan the front anyway,' French said softly. 'We might get away with it.'

It was almost 9 p.m. when I went home. I made myself a cup of coffee and fed the cats. Something was nagging at me but I couldn't reach inside and grab it for inspection. With nothing else to do, I went to my filing cabinet and pulled Ethel's folder. Inside, among the notes and pictures, was a small cassette.

It was a copy of the interview recorded by the police after the murders of Agnes Veronia and PC Richard Bealey. Morris had given it to Don as a favour. I took Sue's Walkman from the mantel shelf and settled the headphones over my ears. The tape was some way through and the first words I heard were, 'Did you see the killer? His face?' That was Ray

Morris. I listened for several seconds and suddenly I heard Ethel say a simple phrase that chilled me to the bone. DI Fletcher asked her if there was anything else about the killer that might help.

'No ... perhaps. Two rose bushes planted close together in a garden. They're important to him ...'

I wound it back to the beginning and listened again. Ethel spoke of the killer's regret at killing the policeman and mentioned a hanged man.

It couldn't be Martin Dunn! He was with me when I rescued Mary White. But the roses? What were the colours? White and yellow? No, yellow with pinkish edging and reddish. I rang Ethel.

She answered almost at once, her voice shaking.

'Are you all right?' I asked.

'There is a huge mob gathering in the street outside,' she said. 'They are armed with bottles and stones and ... swords, I think. It's terrible, Jeremy. They are making a barricade by overturning cars.'

'Keep your door locked and turn off all lights in rooms facing the street,' I told her. 'Now listen, there's something very important. You remember when you talked about the killer having two rose bushes planted close together?'

'Yes.'

'What colour were they?'

'I can do better than that, Jeremy. One was Silver Jubilee, the other Apache.'

'It's the colours I'm after, Ethel. Just the colours.'

'Silver Jubilee is yellowish with pink edges. Apache is red or dark pink.'

'Oh my God!'

'What's wrong?'

'I saw them today. The roses. And I told the man all about you, and how you would catch him.'

'You'd better telephone the police, Jeremy.'

'As soon as I hang up. Keep your door locked. Get Mr Sutcliffe to stay with you.' I replaced the receiver. It couldn't be Martin. There had to be another explanation. I'd just met him outside in his car when the scream came. It was nonsense.

But why was he there in the first place?

It wasn't my problem. I dialled the station but there was no reply. And there was nothing else I could do.

Sue came in just after midnight. She was exhausted.

'God, it's hell out there, Jem. The police won't let us get close. Andrew and Phil are interviewing some of the officers. And it's so hot – there's condensation on the outside of windows, just like on a summer's night. What's wrong? You feeling ill?'

I told her about Martin, and the roses. 'You said his father killed himself and Martin found the body. How did he die?'

'He hanged himself,' said Sue.

'Jesus wept! He's the killer.'

'That's ridiculous,' she said. 'Martin's a lovely man ...' She hesitated.

'What?'

'It was him who told me about the mask in the station.'

'How did he know?'

'Well, once I knew it was Bowyer they'd arrested, it was obvious. Bowyer's current wife is Martin's sister. They're very close. I told the police that but I don't think I ever told you; it was while we weren't speaking.'

'Then he planted the mask and needle.'

'Have you told the police?'

'I can't get through. Everyone must be on riot duty.'

'What will you do?'

I closed my eyes. Once more, the memory of Mr Sutcliffe came hurtling back to me, the night he turned up at my flat. I made a promise then, so lightly given. I swore to protect Ethel, with my life if necessary. I'd learned so much about myself these last few months, my selfishness and my insecurities. Ethel had told me I was a latent psychic. I believed it now. Because in my heart of hearts I knew I was going to die that night.

'I have to get to Ethel's flat. I told Dunn about her.'

'I still don't understand,' she said. 'He was with you when Mary White was attacked.'

'It all makes sense now. Look at the notes. Ambidextrous killer? He's not ambidextrous. There are two of them.'

'You'll never get to Ethel's. That's where the riot is.'

'I haven't any choice. Is the car downstairs?'

'I'll come with you.'

'Not bloody likely. You keep ringing the police.'

She protested but I took the keys and sprinted down the stairs. Outside, sirens wailed in the distance. I drove south, and cut through Trellis Way, getting as close to Lansdowne as I could. Sue was right; the night was unnaturally warm and muggy. Two policemen tried to wave me down but I steered around them and made it another half-mile before I came up against the police lines. Officers in helmets and masks, bearing riot shields, had formed a wall across the road. Before them was a line of burning cars. I skidded the Fiesta to a stop and climbed out.

'Where the hell do you think you're going?' shouted an officer.

I ignored him and ran for the block of flats some two hundred yards across the waste ground. A mob was gathering there, collecting jagged stones for ammunition. They ignored me as I passed. I moved through the ground-floor landing and out into the square beyond, where another thirty-odd youths were filling milk bottles with petrol and rags. Beyond the flats was Cardigan Road. I was breathless now, but still running. Only another few minutes and I would be at Ethel's home. Cardigan Road was deserted, an oasis of grim calm within the riot area. I could run no further. I stopped by a car and leaned on the bonnet, trying to catch my breath. Sweat dripped into my eyes. I wiped it away.

'Oh no!' I whispered.

The car I was leaning on was Martin's silver-grey Jag.

They were already there.

36

Mr Sutcliffe sat in his darkened front room, watching the mob gather, his warrior's eyes automatically separating the leaders from the excited crowd. He observed them directing groups, leading charges against the police line at the other end of Church Path, or organising the destruction of walls and the ripping up of paving slabs to gather missiles.

Mangiwe Mazui had seen many such riots in Bulawayo. There, however, they would have been put down by armed police and the days following marked by funerals. Many youngsters outside were wearing balaclava masks, or scarves tied round their faces, and such was the degree of lust and violence within the mob that Mr Sutcliffe closed the curtains, both on the windows of his house and the windows of his talent.

In the darkness he sat, his eyes drawn by the faintest spear of lamplight from the street to the assegai on the chimney breast. With that blade, he had killed his first lion and wounded his first enemy.

Tonight, with luck, it would drink one last time.

The noise outside was deafening. He stood and opened the curtains. It was hard to see through the condensation – which was ... outside? Mangiwe opened the window and leaned out. The air was still. High in the sky, the clouds were racing, but here all was supernaturally calm.

Mangiwe shook his head. Tonight. The Devil Wind would come tonight.

The police were charging the mob around eighty yards away, and cars were being dragged across the road and overturned. A young boy lit the rag in his Molotov cocktail and waited for the rioters to withdraw. Then he hurled it at the line of cars.

'Fool!' whispered Mangiwe Mazui. He retreated to the back bedroom and waited. One minute later, three explosions shook the old terraced house to its foundations. Mangiwe ran to the living room. The windows had shattered, the curtains were on fire. He tore them down and shoved them through the broken glass, where they lay smouldering on his rose bushes. In the street, the youth who had thrown the petrol bomb was writhing as his body blazed. Around him, several men were vainly slapping his burning form with coats. Mangiwe ran to the bedroom and gathered up a blanket. He went to the boy and smothered the flames swiftly and expertly.

The youngster's tortured eyes opened, registering the immense pain. He screamed once and died. A pistol shot sounded from Beverley Towers. Mangiwe stood, the smell of scorched flesh acrid in his nostrils. Across the road, the grocer's shop was burning. At the upstairs window stood a little girl, struggling to open the catch.

A black youth ran to the shopfront and began to climb the drainpipe beside the door. Mr Sutcliffe walked across to stand beneath the boy, ready to catch him if he fell. The youth reached the window and smashed it with his fist before knocking out all the shards. The child refused his pleas to climb onto the sill. The flames behind her licked at her nightdress, which erupted in flame. The boy scrambled through the window, tearing the clothing from her even as his own jumper smouldered and burned. Taking the girl in his arms, he climbed onto the sill again.

'Drop her!' shouted Mr Sutcliffe. The boy did so, the child screaming as he let go. Mr Sutcliffe caught her and spun, feeling the muscles of his back rip with the weight. He groaned and put her down. As the boy swung on to the drainpipe, it sagged outwards. He lost his balance and fell.

Mr Sutcliffe threw his body under the boy, trying to take the weight across his arms. The boy hit him hard and the two crashed to the ground. Mr Sutcliffe rolled to his knees, blanking out the pain. The boy's hands were blistered and bleeding, and the hairs had been burned from his eyebrows.

'Can you walk?' asked Mr Sutcliffe.

The boy nodded. Mr Sutcliffe gathered the crying child and led the way back to his house.

'What is your name?' he asked the youth as they sat in the back bedroom, the girl curled foetally in the bed, too frightened to sleep.

'Justin Richards.'

'I am Mr Sutcliffe. What you did was very brave. And now you must continue with your courage,' he said, pointing to Justin's burned hands. 'You must accept the pain, blend with it. This child's life is in your hands. You have made a bond. Sit with her. She will need someone close.'

'Her parents were still inside—'

'I know, but you did what you could.' Mr Sutcliffe leaned over the child, touching his huge hand to her cheek. 'Sleep, little one. You are safe among friends.' He bent and kissed her brow. Her eyelids fluttered and her gaze flicked to Justin, who smiled at her. Finally, she slept.

Mr Sutcliffe took his assegai from the wall and walked through the kitchen into the yard beyond and out into the garden facing the small recreation park. He sucked in a great gulp of air, tasting the petrol fumes and the burning rubber. The noise from the street was less raucous here. He opened his mind to the night, seeking his star. He glanced at Ethel's house three gardens down.

They had enjoyed a morning coffee only a few hours ago, and talked of life and love and dreams. Mr Sutcliffe, in a rare moment of embarrassment, had given her his talisman box. She had made to open it but he stopped her.

'No,' he said softly. 'When I have gone. There is much of my life in there. Several photographs, a medal or two and some letters I wrote to you but never sent. Read them ... when I am ... no longer here. As for the rest, you will learn of me through them.'

She had cried then, and for the first time he held her, stroking her hair. He looked up, seeking his star, but the clouds were bunching now. The wind gusted and the trees rustled, bending and swaying as if panicked by the sudden change in the weather. A great roaring drowned out the noise of the riot. Mangiwe stretched his arms out to the sky, the assegai shining with dark light.

Gary Sinclair pulled his mask into place and stepped from the shadows of the trees at the rear of the garden. He could see the old black man now, and he grinned as he noticed the spear. He raised the Colt and took careful aim. The first shot hammered into the man's chest, punching him back several steps. He staggered but lurched upright, turning to face his attacker. Sinclair's second shot missed but his third hit home. His target roared his defiance – and charged.

In that moment, as the wind howled and branches were torn from the trees around him, Sinclair's dreams hurtled back into mind. *The black lion! Oh my God! It's Sutcliffe!*

Sinclair took the revolver in both hands and emptied it into the charging man.

Mangiwe's eyes focused on the man in a black mask with the word DEATH embroidered on it in white. He was standing by the tree ten yards away, pointing a revolver. Mangiwe screamed and charged. Another bullet struck him. And another. The charge faltered and he slipped, the last shell whistling by his head. Mangiwe bunched his muscles beneath him, feeling death calling him from the void. He threw himself over the last few feet, his hands tearing at the figure before him. The gun barrel lashed down across his face but he ignored it, his left hand curling around the throat, feeling the coarseness of the balaclava wool, his right sweeping up, driving the assegai deep into his killer's belly.

Waves of dizziness overtook him but he hurled them back, fighting for the last second of life. His massive hand twisted the haft of the spear, the blade disembowelling his enemy. Mangiwe fell and rolled to his back, his body alive with roaring heat and pain.

Suddenly he was in the bush again, wounded and alone, bleeding from the wounds in his lower back, and the lion was rushing from the bushes. Mangiwe's Kalashnikov bucked in his hand, sending four bullets into the beast. Yet still it came, even as he just had against the masked killer. Mangiwe had drawn his serrated hunting knife, his left hand grabbing the lion's mane to hold the slavering jaws from his face. He curled his legs around the beast's body, preventing it from using its lethal hind claws, then stabbed it over and over again. He had never forgotten the sight of those yellow-gold eyes staring into his own in those dreadful moments, nor the savage joy he felt when he watched the light fade from them as the great beast sank beside him in death. He knew then that the lion's soul had merged with his own, and its great strength had flowed into him. And he remembered his own exultant cry.

'I am Mangiwe Mazui – and I shall live for ever!'

As he lay looking up at the storm-torn sky, for a moment the clouds parted and he saw his star, so bright and so distant.

The grass was cool against his neck, and the pain eased.

Someone was kneeling beside him. His head turned.

'You bastard,' said Martin Dunn, lifting the six-inch needle.

But Mangiwe Mazui had passed beyond his reach. Even so, Dunn plunged the needle again and again into the dead man's chest.

Then he climbed the garden fence and headed towards the end house.

Four hours had passed since the first action and Beverley Towers was ominously quiet. All the people from the surrounding flats on the fourth storey had left the building. Only the policemen and the dead remained. Fletcher ordered the bodies covered with blankets, then lit one of his remaining cigarettes.

Adams was sitting in a brown vinyl armchair, toying with his gun. His face was grey and taut with fear.

'Put the gun away,' said Fletcher.

'Sorry, sir, what was that?'

'I said, put the gun away.' He turned to a constable. 'Walker?'

'Yes, sir,' said the officer.

'See if there's any tea or coffee left in the kitchen.'

The other three uniformed men were on the landing outside the flat, watching for any sign of attack. Fletcher drew deeply on his cigarette, enjoying the warmth in his throat and lungs. He was worried about Adams, who looked on the edge of panic. He sat down beside him.

'Did you find out about a cleaning woman?'

'What?'

'The Bowyer house? Come on, man, snap out of it!'

'Oh yes. Name's Mrs Reynolds. Comes in Wednesdays and Fridays.'

'She remember any visitors this week?'

'The insurance man, the window cleaner and Mrs Bowyer's brother, Martin.'

'Martin who?'

'Martin Dunn, the guy who owns the computer business.'

'What do we know about him?'

'Nice guy, by all accounts. Donates to local charities, that sort of thing. Gay.'

'I hate that word, Adams. Gay means happy, lively. Homosexual is the word you're looking for.'

'Whatever, sir.'

Fletcher watched in sorrow as the glazed look returned to Adams's eyes. He stretched and saw his own reflection in the full-size mirror on the far wall. Reflection? What had Ethel Hurst said about something being wrong? Like looking in a mirror. Everything the wrong way round? Left becoming right. Fletcher's mouth was dry and he licked his lips. The reflection followed suit. What had Ethel seen in that dreadful moment? Not a mirror reflection. No. Two figures, identical, save that one was left-handed, the other right-handed. Two killers.

And Martin Dunn was connected to the Bowyers, and had been close by when Mary White was attacked. Maybe that's why the killer got in so easily the second time. It wouldn't have taken much for Martin to palm the keys while he was there.

Damn you, Fletcher, you should have seen it. So who's the other one?

Martin was homosexual, and Gary Sinclair had a conviction for gross indecency. Fletcher would bet his pension on them being lovers.

Outside, PC Pierce yawned. Earlier, his adrenaline had been firing on all cylinders as they waited for the inevitable attack. But it hadn't materialised and the officer, who had been on duty since six that morning, was beginning to feel mortally weary. He was cold, and a howling storm was raging over the estate, the wind lashing rain onto the landing.

He stifled a yawn and saw a hand appear over the parapet. As Pierce walked forward to investigate, a man heaved himself over and onto the landing.

'Where do you think you're going?' said Pierce. Then he saw the sawn-off shotgun. He tried to dive to the left but the blast took him full in the chest and he was catapulted back. PC Walker had just come from the flat bearing three cups of scalding black coffee. He leapt forward and flung the burning liquid into the gunman's face. The man screamed. Walker dropped the empty cups and hammered a fist into the man's face. He toppled backwards and plunged sixty feet to the courtyard below.

At that moment, the swing doors at either end of the landing opened and the mob surged through, bearing ripped-off doors before them as shields.

'Mr Fletcher!' yelled Walker.

Fletcher heard the shotgun and ran out into the open. 'Get back in the flat!' he shouted.

'What about Pierce?'

Fletcher took in the still body and shook his head. 'He's dead.'

The officers moved back inside and wedged the door shut as best they could. It had already been smashed inwards when they tried to take Seymour Holding and what was left of it wouldn't last long against the mob now pushing at the fractured wood.

Fletcher fired a shot high through a crack at the top of the door. The crowd scattered.

'All in all,' said Walker, 'I think I'd rather supervise a Chelsea match.'

Fletcher grinned. 'Even Chelsea v Arsenal?'

'No, sir. In that instance, I'd sooner be here.'

'Move the bodies and barricade this hallway,' said Fletcher.

The officers hauled the corpses into the main bedroom then dragged a chest of drawers into the hall and pushed it tightly against the door.

Through all this activity, Adams remained where he was, sitting in the armchair staring at his gun. Fletcher went to him and gently eased the weapon from his fingers.

'I didn't mean to kill the boy,' said Adams, tears in his eyes.

'I know that, John. Sit there quietly.'

The door to the second bedroom flew open and three men ran into the living room. Fletcher hurled himself at the first, smashing the barrel of Adams's gun across the man's forehead, stunning him. The blade of a machete crashed down on his shoulder and bounced off and he fell, dropping the weapon. Walker charged the attackers, his truncheon cracking against the third man's skull. Fletcher swept up the gun and fired. The bullet took the machete-wielder in the leg, smashing his thigh. Walker and the two other officers forced their way into the bedroom where four more men had climbed the fire escape and entered through the back window.

Yet more were trying to clamber through. Walker yelled at the top of his voice and charged. The four men were armed with knives, but the speed and ferocity of the officer's attack paralysed them. His truncheon crashed down, bowling two of them from their feet. The others ran for the window. Walker let them go.

Fletcher stumbled in alongside him, blood seeping from his smashed shoulder.

'Well done, Walker.'

'Bloody stupid to miss that fire escape,' he said. 'And I've changed my mind, sir. I'd sooner have Chelsea-Arsenal.'

'I'll bear that in mind. But for now you'd better handcuff the prisoners.'

'Many more attacks, sir, and we'll run out of handcuffs.'

Fletcher tried to answer, but his knees buckled and darkness swallowed him.

Outside, the storm vented its fury. Windows exploded, a tree crashed onto the barricade in Church Path, and the mob scattered before the rage of nature.

37

He stood outside the terraced flat, his mind in turmoil. It had all gone so wrong. The only man he had ever loved – apart from dad – was dead, and to safeguard himself he had to kill an elderly woman. His throat was dry.

The great adventure was coming to a close. How arrogant it felt now, those early nights of planning in the spring, when Gary found out about Jack Bowyer's affair with Barbara Sinclair. Poor Gary had been heartbroken. Not just because the bitch was still screwing around – he'd never got over that – but because she'd shared his secret with Bowyer. That terrible time after the arrest, when his life had been in shreds.

'You're an impotent little cocksucker,' she'd told him that time they met at a party. 'Shagged any nice men lately?'

'I wish I could kill her,' Gary had said as they lay in bed together. For Martin, the idea had genuine charm. He hated Jack Bowyer for what he was, a bed-hopping betrayer, nowhere near good enough for his sister. How his antics hurt her! Just as Martin's mother had destroyed his father. Now it was happening again, with Bowyer wrecking his sister's life. She couldn't see it. But Bowyer would leave her, and then, maybe, it would be like Dad all over again, only this time it would be Wendy hanging from the banister rail.

'We can kill her, Gary,' he said that fateful night.

'The police would be here so fast my feet wouldn't touch the ground.'

'I could kill her. While you're in Amsterdam. But you'd have to do something for me.'

'What?'

'Help me nail Bowyer.'

'How?'

'Kill his ex-wife.'

'No way, Marry. We're bound to get caught.'

'Not if we're clever. And we are. And you do want her dead, don't you?'

It took him weeks to convince Gary. But he did. Gary still had the copy of the *Herald* with his wedding photograph, and it had been glorious fun tracking down the other bitches who had ruined men.

But now it was ashes. Gary was dead. Martin couldn't believe how the giant had kept coming, his body almost blown apart by the shells from Gary's gun.

Stop thinking about it! You're alive. And you'll come out of this smelling of roses. They'll find Gary and they'll think he killed the old lady as well as her friend. They'll close the case. You'll be free.

Free? He had never been free. Not since the day he'd found Dad.

He settled his balaclava mask in place and moved forward, testing the back door. It was open. He entered the darkened kitchen and walked along the carpeted hallway. There was a light showing under a door on the right.

Slowly, he turned the handle and stepped inside. An elderly woman was sitting in an old armchair, working slowly at a ring of cloth she was embroidering. She looked up, registering no surprise.

'I have been expecting you,' she said.

He didn't reply. He gripped the cork handle tightly and advanced towards her.

*

The raging storm tore at me as I forced my way along Cardigan Road. Slates hissed by, borne on the wings of a terrible wind. A tree across the road suddenly lurched and split, crashing down on a parked car. The noise was deafening. Close by, I saw a window shatter but could hear no sound of breaking glass. It was like the end of the world. I slipped and fell several times, and once a sharp slate flashed by my head and buried itself in the trunk of a swaying tree. I was terrified.

The rain came down in sheets, needle-sharp and blinding. I rounded the corner and saw the mob scattering, running for shelter. Another tree groaned and fell, tearing up paving slabs.

I cut across the small recreation park and climbed over the shattered fence at the back of Mr Sutcliffe's garden. I found him lying on the grass, his body torn, his spirit gone. Beside him was a black youth, kneeling and holding his hand.

He looked up as I stumbled through the rain. Here the wind was less fierce.

'They shot him to pieces,' he said, pointing to a second corpse with a black mask. 'But he still managed to kill one of them.'

'He was a strong man.'

'You're Jeremy from the paper, aren't you?'

'Yes. Do I know you?'

'Yeah, but we all look alike, huh?'

'No, I'm just terrible with faces.'

'Justin Richards. I saw you at Dawn Green's house.'

'I remember. The mechanic.'

'You wrote about me scratching cars and giving her the V-sign.'

'Yes. She was quite a woman.'

'I loved her, man. She was great. You going after that other killer or what?'

'Oh my God!' I whispered. I leapt up and vaulted the fence, scrambling across the rose beds and two more fences. Ethel's back door was open, the house dark and forbidding. I moved inside, my heart thumping like a drum.

There was a light in the hall, beaming from a side room. Thunder roared outside.

'I've been expecting you,' I heard Ethel say as I ran into the room.

The killer swung, the needle lancing my shoulder as I hammered into him. There was no pain, and I fought like a madman, my fists cracking into his face, but I've never been a fighter. He rolled away and turned, his right foot thundering into my belly. The air whooshed from my lungs and I stumbled. He spun and his left foot crashed against my temple, hurling me into a wall. I was dazed but fighting mad. I lunged at him and the needle speared my chest. I used to read about people describing 'stabbing pains'. It's strange, but it's like being kicked by a mule. There's no sensation of being pierced, just an immense, rounded pain that explodes from within. I sank to the floor, lost and dying.

I couldn't move. He knelt beside me, the awful mask close to my face. The needle, dripping blood, rose until it was just above my right eye.

'Stop that!' said Ethel softly. He looked around. From under the embroidery on her lap she lifted a large black pistol.

The killer slowly stood. 'Now what?' came the voice of Martin Dunn, muffled by the wool.

'They killed Mr Sutcliffe,' I whispered.

'I know, dear. I felt his passing. He is at peace.'

Martin Dunn pulled the mask from his face. 'Well,' he said, 'looks like I'm for it now.'

'You are an evil man,' said Ethel. 'I have never met the likes of you.'

'Oh, spare me the lectures,' snapped Martin. 'Call the police.'

'That won't be necessary,' said Ethel.

'You're letting me go?'

'In a manner of speaking. I was born in a different age, young man. We all seemed to know back then what was wrong and what was right. We strived to be good people. To be caring. But we were harsh in other ways. We knew what punishment was. We accepted it, and we dished it out when it was necessary. Do you understand what I'm saying?'

'You can't mean to kill me. You can't!'

'No, Ethel!' I said, struggling to stand.

'Stay still, Jeremy,' she said. I glanced at her then and saw the flinty look in her eyes, the hard set to her jaw. 'Let me explain something to you,' she told Dunn. 'I am not normally a vengeful person, but three times I have died because of you, and because of the man who shot Mr Sutcliffe. I haven't merely seen your evil. I have lived it, and I have endured it. The souls of Barbara Sinclair and Dorothy Bowyer and Agnes Veronia all touched mine. My life rhymed with theirs in that most awful of moments, when their eyes read the message on your mask. This is not vengeance. This is justice.'

The gun came up.

'Please …' begged Martin. 'I didn't kill all of them. Only the bitch queen and the suicide. I swear to God …'

'Do it in person,' said Ethel. She pulled the trigger.

And nothing happened. Martin leapt forward, tearing the weapon from her grasp.

Suddenly he laughed. 'You forgot the safety catch, Mrs Hurst.' He swung the pistol to point at her face.

'Indeed I did,' said Ethel, calmly. 'And now you are free to wreak your evil.'

'No last words?' asked Martin Dunn, extending his arm so that the gun barrel rested against Ethel's brow. I struggled to move but my legs were like jelly.

'Don't do it, Martin. She's not your mother!'

Martin swung on me. 'Shut up! What do you know about it?'

'Your father was a fine man,' said Ethel. 'He tried so hard. But he could never understand why you liked to kill things, could he? And when you strangled that little girl behind the old factory, he just gave up. He killed himself and left a note for the police, telling them all about you and your murderous ways.'

Martin turned slowly towards her, the gun forgotten.

'It wasn't me,' he said. 'It was a tramp. The police looked everywhere for him.'

'But your father knew it was you. It was the final straw for him.'

'No! It was the bitch! You don't know anything!'

'Be a good boy, Martin,' said Ethel, softly. 'Isn't that what Daddy used to say? Be a good boy and make me proud of you. But you had to kill, didn't you? Pets first, and then people.'

Martin backed away towards the door. 'It wasn't me! It wasn't!'

'Be a good boy, Martin.'

Martin Dunn ran from the room and out into the deserted, storm-torn street. The rain lashed him and he stopped.

Don't let her fool you, the witch. Kill her. KILL HER!

He turned back to the house.

Fletcher was in terrible pain by the time reinforcements arrived, but he brightened when Walker offered him a cigarette.

'I had no idea you were a smoker. Why didn't you tell me you had cigarettes?'

'You never asked me, sir. How's the shoulder?'

'Hurts like hell.'

'Well, you know what they used to say – "Dull it isn't."'

'God, you're older than you look, Walker.'

'You're not, sir.'

Fifteen minutes later, an ambulance arrived. It was 4.35 a.m. Fletcher swore as he was being lifted into the back.

'What is it, sir?' asked Walker.

'There!' said Fletcher, pointing to the grey Jag. 'Shit! That's Dunn's car. Get me out.'

'You're injured, sir. Relax!'

'Get me out!' roared Fletcher. PC Walker half-lifted him from the stretcher and the inspector took a deep breath to steady himself. 'End house,' he said, staggering off towards the row of terraces. Walker ran after him.

'Will you at least tell me what's going on, sir?' shouted Walker, trying to make himself heard above the storm. A slate crashed into the road, spraying fragments. One caught Fletcher above the right eye. 'This is madness!' yelled Walker.

'Deathmask!' screamed Fletcher. 'He's after the psychic!'

At that moment, Martin Dunn ran from the house, gun in hand. Fletcher was thirty feet away.

'Dunn!' he yelled. The wind dropped. 'Dunn!'

Martin whirled, saw the police uniform and fired. The bullet punched through the top of Walker's helmet, singeing his hair. Fletcher raised his own gun and pulled the trigger. The shot took Martin high in the chest, spinning him. Fletcher cocked his pistol and ran forward.

'It's over!' he screamed. 'Give it up!'

Dunn's arm whipped up. Fletcher fired again. Martin sagged to his knees, but once more raised the gun. Fletcher stood and waited.

Martin stared at the detective, then at the police constable who was running to join him. Ethel appeared in the doorway and walked slowly towards him.

'Be a good boy, Martin,' she said. 'Do the right thing.'

Blood bubbled from Martin's lips. Ethel knelt beside him. The pistol came up.

A single shot sounded and Martin Dunn pitched back, a bullet in his brain.

Ethel stood and walked to Fletcher. 'The other one is in Mr Sutcliffe's garden. They killed him.' Ethel looked to the sky, which was rapidly clearing. 'The Devil Wind has gone,' she said. 'And you should be getting to hospital. Jeremy's inside and he's badly hurt. Can you bring the ambulance here? Then you can both be patched up.'

'You're a remarkable lady, Mrs Hurst,' said Fletcher.

Ethel smiled. 'If only that were true.'

'Take his word for it, madam,' said PC Walker. 'He can be vile when people don't agree with him.'

38

I was in hospital for three weeks with a punctured lung, and people visited me every day, bringing grapes, oranges, even flowers. What with Mother and Sue and Don Bateman coming in, I began to long for the sanctuary of my flat. Sue was looking after my cats.

On the fifth day of my incarceration, Ethel came to visit.

'How did you know all that about the girl he strangled, and the pets?' I asked her.

'When he wrestled the gun from me, our hands touched. They were terrible images, Jeremy. His was a soul in torment. But he didn't have the strength to accept the blame for his father's death, so he destroyed his suicide note and blamed his mother. But he killed again long before the Deathmask business. A young hitchhiker in Greece, a girl in Miami. He couldn't stop himself.'

'Would you really have killed him?'

'Oh yes. I feel so stupid about missing the safety catch.'

During the second week, Don came in with great news. In Buffalo, New York, Dr Chan had finally performed surgery on Stan King. They had found – almost by accident, apparently – that the cancer had only pierced the outer fleshy layer of the heart. When they cut it away, the rest of Stan's heart was fine. They could treat his windpipe. The cancer was gone, and Stan could begin to lead a normal life again.

I almost cried. It felt like the perfect ending.

I went home alone on a Saturday morning. I could hear Mrs Simcox moving about in her flat, the chink of her glass against the bottle, the springs in her chair as she sat.

I knocked on her door. She answered it, her sad eyes questioning.

'Hello, Mrs Simcox. Just thought I'd tell you I'm home.'

'I could put the kettle on,' she said, as she always did, knowing the inevitable answer.

'Please do,' I said. 'I'd love to sit and chat.'

AFTERWORD BY STAN NICHOLLS

I loved my mother. When she died, after four years ravaged by cancer, I couldn't cry. I wasn't being callous. As I said, I loved her. It's just that I've never been easily given to tears, whatever the circumstances and however I felt. At David Gemmell's funeral I wept. Maybe that says something about me. But as I was far from alone I think it says everything about Dave Gemmell.

How 'autobiographical' is *Rhyming Rings*? Readers who know something of the author's life will say quite a bit. When protagonist Jeremy Miller is introduced we're given a basic description – *'The man was tall, his hair close cropped and neat.'* – and that certainly matched Gemmell's appearance. The setting is West London, where Gemmell grew up. Jeremy's a journalist, working on a local newspaper, as Gemmell did. He's depicted as arrogant and sure of his supposed brilliance, while at the same time finding it hard to express emotions. By Gemmell's own admission that's a fairly accurate portrait of himself at twenty-four.

Jeremy's despondent about gentrification sweeping away closely-knit communities and the loss of a collective social responsibility. I think it's fair to say that Gemmell was troubled by that too. At one point, Jeremy says of journalists,

'... *Most people think we're cynics, because we mock and we see through the posturings of politicians, the shallow greed of businessmen, and the many and varied faults and flaws of a material society. But we are not natural cynics. We enter journalism because of our ideals, marching in as romantics who think we can change the world.'* I believe that's pretty much how Gemmell saw his role as a journalist. And would it be too fanciful to see that desire to 'change the world', if just a little, in his fantasy novels?

Jeremy Miller is on the right, politically. His lover, Sue Cater, is on the left. Some of the things Jeremy says – about attitudes to criminality and what you might call moral accountability – echo the author, who was in some respects socially conservative. Other aspects don't. Jeremy's unthinking, almost childish homophobia and the racist attitudes of various characters in no way reflect Gemmell's world-view. In fact, in laying bare the bigotry he exposes it for what it is.

I don't think Gemmell was political in a party sense, more pick 'n' mix, basing his opinions on his own moral compass rather than dogma. Pleasingly, you could disagree and argue with him without it affecting friendship, something we seem to have largely lost in the age of social media.

Dawn Green, Mister Sutcliffe and the psychic, Ethel Hurst, are religious, or at least spiritual in nature. Jeremy isn't. That's a difference, given Gemmell's Christianity. But Jeremy's transition from jerk to hero, to a kind of redemption, could be said to reflect Gemmell's own journey as he navigated the faith he'd chosen, with the doubts and questions I imagine all religious people have. Or am I reading too much into it?

Certain asides in the novel are consciously self-referential. Tolkien and *The Lord of the Rings* are mentioned, and Conan. We're told that Jeremy has a collection of *Spider-Man* comics. Most tellingly, he's trying to write a book: *'... I was creating the perfect novel, a grim fantasy about a giant barbarian hacking his way through a savage world.*

Naturally he had muscles like hawser cables, women found him irresistible, and his enemies fell like wheat before a scythe.' This epic's hero, Borak, could be a rough sketch, or maybe a parody, of Druss, the popular character introduced in *Legend* (1984), Gemmell's debut fantasy novel.

There are other references that seem to touch the author's life. For example, Jeremy says, '*My first job had been as a lorry driver's mate, delivering soft drinks to cafés. There was more money in it, and fewer hours. Still, lorry drivers rarely had the chance to track down murderers.*' This calls to mind a rejection letter Gemmell received in the early 1960s, which he often quoted when giving talks. It ended, '*You mention in your resume that you are working as a lorry driver's mate for Pepsi Cola. This is an occupation not without merit. Good luck with it.*'

Jeremy also has a collection of American civil war soldiers. '*My heroes were the Confederates,*' he explains. '*Not, I hasten to add, because I liked the idea of slavery. No, I just have a soft spot for losers.*' You have echoes of *Legend* and the Alamo, which partly inspired it, right there. As a rider to this, mention should be made of the peripheral character Stan King in *Rhyming Rings*, who appears to have terminal cancer, in light of the fact that an incorrect diagnosis of cancer was what drove Gemmell to finish *Legend* in record time.

Playing spot the reference is fun, but less important than how well *Rhyming Rings* stands up as a thriller. We know from various allusions in the text, and the climatic storm, that the novel is set in 1987, although it was probably written a few years later. In that respect it's almost an historical. Racial tensions and riots were headline news at the time, street robberies peaked, local newspapers had healthy circulations and absolutely *everyone* smoked. The IT we take for granted didn't exist – when a computer plays a minor role it seems exotic in this context. But we don't mind the absence of mobiles, Googling or other modern conveniences, any more than we do in a Ngaio Marsh, Dashell Hammett or Raymond Chandler novel. Because storytelling trumps props, and Gemmell had that skill in abundance.

He was one of those people who have a natural talent – maybe predilection would be a better word – for making up stories and for writing. I've known few other people who found writing such a comfortable process. I'm not saying it was easy or he didn't work hard; of course he did. But I'd be surprised if he broke a sweat. His work practices, and aspects of his style, can be attributed to his years as a journalist. Journalism teaches you to express yourself clearly, economically and with impact. It trains you to get the job done. The upshot in Gemmell's case is crisp, pacey narratives with strong plots and a lack of clutter. But there's something else – an enviable ability to convey a lot of emotion in a minimum number of words. It's characteristic of his work, and what he more than once referred to as the 'magic' in the writing process.

Leaving aside the argument that all fiction is fantasy, given that fiction can only be an approximation of reality, there are definite thematic similarities in Gemmell's crime and fantasy novels. Initially, Jeremy is a poser (a word Gemmell was happy to apply to himself in a typically self-deprecating way) and his swagger makes him unpopular, not unlike Rek in *Legend*. Some aspects of Jeremy's personality – his outbursts of temper, for instance – are distinctly unattractive. Yet he winds up doing the right thing. This 'shades of grey' characterisation is something Gemmell applied to many of his characters, heroes and villains alike, giving his casts a believable reality.

Mister Sutcliffe, the giant capable of murder, and Ethel,

the psychic, are ageing, and in the case of Sutcliffe his resilience is starting to wane. This mirrors a running theme in Gemmell's work – the weakening of a warrior's powers in the face of advancing years – as definitively embodied in Druss the Axeman.

A rare but not unknown departure for Gemmell in *Rhyming Rings* in terms of structure is his use of a point of view that switches from first to third person throughout. This can be risky, but here it works. I can't help but wonder if he employed his less rare practice of drawing any of the characters from real life. That got him into trouble in 1986, with the publication of his third novel, *Waylander*, in which several of his newspaper colleagues were used as characters. '*The managing director regarded it as a poisonous attack on his integrity,*' Gemmell said later. It cost him his job.

There's humour in all of Gemmell's work, albeit often gallows. And it tends to have an appealing dryness, as in the exchange, about how life had gone downhill, between Mister Sutcliffe and Ethel:

'*… You had no evil eye then,*' *he said, pointing to the television.*

'*I hardly think Crossroads encourages muggers,*' *said Ethel.*

I suspect that might have been a little wave to Gemmell's long-standing friend and *Crossroads* co-creator Peter Ling.

It's wonderful to have a 'new' Gemmell book to read when you thought everything was known. My only regret is that *Rhyming Rings* wasn't published at the time it was written. We don't know why that was. But sound storytelling is timeless, and even now the book holds its own against the graphic content of much contemporary crime fiction. An unblinking look at horrors like a masked man appearing at the foot of your bed in the middle of the night is nightmarish in any decade.

On the day my mother died I spoke to Dave Gemmell on the phone. He was, of course, sympathetic and supportive. First thing next morning there was a letter from him in the post. I don't know, but maybe he found it easier to express himself in writing. In it, he spoke of his feelings when his own mother died, what the loss meant to him, and the value of keeping loved ones alive in our memories. And, dammit, he delivered this great big, kind, compassionate, emotional wallop on one sheet of A4, which I treasure. More of that Gemmell magic.

Tears were the least we owed him.